BURNIN' RUBBER

THE Remembrances OF AN OLD MAN

DEDICATION

This book is dedicated to anyone and everyone who ever loved their car. If you believe that your ride was more than just transportation. If you gave your car a name and the very best tender lovin' care possible.

You've probably got more than blood pumping through your veins, you've got a higher octane level than the average man or woman on the street.

You understood the importance of keeping her clean at all times, waxing her under a shade tree on Sunday afternoon. Keeping her finely tuned and all her fluid levels topped off.

You took care of her and she took care of you, you depended on each other.

Her radio was always tuned into that old time Rock n' Roll and her duel exhaust always sounded so fine.

If you can related to anything I've just said, This book is dedicated to YOU.

FORWARD

This is a story about hot rods and hot rodding. It's also a story about girls, high school and that good old time rock n' roll music of the 50's and 60's.

Even more importantly, this is the story about the life and times of this great nation. The good times and the bad, I have white washed nothing and I haven't over glamorized anything either, I didn't have to.

This is my story you're reading but I sincerely hope that you find yourself in many of these pages.

I was born in 1943 during the world's great struggle against domination and tyranny. However, this is not a story about war, even though it seems like America has been in one war or another my whole life.

This is the story of America's love of the automobile or at least my undying obsession with cars, especially hot rods and custom built cars.

Chapter One

'The Happy Days'

When the Second World War ended in 1945, hundreds of thousands of GI's came home to find a totally new world awaiting them. While they were gone, their wives and girlfriends had grown and matured into stronger more confident women.

There was a housing and manufacturing boom like never before. Jobs were in abundance and any man or woman who wanted to work, had his or her pick of jobs. Thousands of GI's went back to school under the newly developed GI Bill passed by congress. Many more by the hundreds headed for Detroit, Michigan.

In Detroit, they were manufacturing tens of thousands of automobiles and trucks each year. These new motor vehicles were relatively inexpensive and something that the masses could afford to own and enjoy.

After having gone through a national depression in the 1930's and a devastating world-wide war in the early 1940's, the late 1940's and 1950's were truly 'The Happy Days' of the Twentieth Century.

Most of the vehicles built from 1946 thru 1948 were basically recycled versions of what they were building before the war had broken out.

Ford and Mercury were offering models with both flathead sixes and a flathead V8. This was a slightly updated 90 horsepower engine that they had originally introduced to the world in 1932 in their 'B' Models, which had a whopping 60 horsepower. Lincoln being a bigger luxury automobile had a V12 flathead engine.

General Motors offered a much larger variety of engines. Chevrolet's were equipped with a babbit bearing, overhead valve engine very similar to the ones that they had been using since 1929. Pontiac and Oldsmobile were using flathead engines as well as Cadillac, except theirs was a V8.

!n 1949 Oldsmobile turns the automotive world upside down by introducing its short stoke, very fast, Overhead Valve V8 engine. With their new

'Rocket' engine and hydromatic transmission, Oldsmobile inadvertently started a 'Horsepower Race' which would become an all-out war.

By 1950 Hollywood was cranking out movies at a fevered pace and with the advent of the outdoor drive-in theatre being in its hay day, there were nearly 4,000 nation-wide. Nearly any town of any size had at least one.

I remember as a child going to these outdoor movies with my whole family. Before the movie began, we children could be found playing on the playground equipment down in front of the huge wide screen. Many of the parents would entertain themselves by chasing each other around on the blank screen with their spotlights.

Until 1952, Oldsmobile had dominated the race tracks but now they were losing races to the 'Fabulous Hudson Hornet'. Hudson had developed its own short stoke highly tuned engine. This engine which Hudson called the 'H Twin' was a flathead six with duel carburetors, duel exhausts and an aluminum high compression racing head.

Buick followed suit with an overhead valve straight eight engine equipped with duel carburetors and duel exhaust as well.

Cadillac being General Motor's luxury car had an overhead valve V8, but it was no race car. This engine had a big bore and long stroke built for highway travel. However as the years went by many of these engines found them tucked into light weight custom built race cars.

Chrysler Corporation which up until 1953 had been happy with their flathead engines launches a revolutionary new engine design. This engine had 'Hemispherical' type heads and quickly became known as 'Hemi' engines. They were high horsepower engines but they were not light weight by any means.

Studebaker also gets into the horsepower race with not one but two new overhead V8s in its new 'sporty' car models. In addition to the Commander series, Studebaker introduces the 'Starlight' and 'Star liner' coupes. These were actually steel bodied sport cars in the truest sense of the word. They were smaller, lighter and built lower to the ground than any car had ever been built before.

Some of these cars actually came equipped with Cadillac V8 engines, which were quickly dubbed ' Studillacs'.

Not to be out done, Chevrolet builds a mass produced fiberglass sports car they called 'The Corvette'. It came complete with bucket seats and a three speed floor mounted transmission shifter. It is powered by a new pressured bearing overhead valve six cylinder engine they call 'The Blue Flame'. This engine Is 235 C.I.D (cubic Inch Displacement) and has three side mounted carburetors.

Fast Cars and home built hot rods could be seen nearly everywhere. They were at not only seen at the drive-in theatres but at the juke joints, malt shops, drive thru fast food restaurants, roller skating rinks, bowling alleys and any other place else where girls and a good time could be found.

Another important ingredient in having a good time included the music of the day, which was what radio disc jockey Alan Freed first coined 'Rock n' Roll'.

Chapter Two

'Youthful Bliss'

I guess that the very first rock n' roll song actually hit the radio waves in 1948. It was a song recorded by Wynonie Harris entitled 'Good Rockin' Tonight'. One of my personal favorites Fats Domino released 'The Fat Man' and 'Boogie Woogie Baby' in 1950.

Jackie Brenston recorded 'Rocket 88' for Leonard Chess of Chess Records in 1951. Making both Oldsmobile and cruising more popular than ever.

Wild Bill Haley and his Comets gave us 'Rock Around the Clock' in 1954 which unleashed dozens of other artists doing rock n' roll music. Hollywood jumped on the bandwagon and produced scores of roll n' roll inspired movies, some good and some not so good.

There were only a couple of things in the 1954 new car season that would put a smile on the faces of auto enthusiasts.

Ford finally enters the world of overhead valve V8s with an engine called the 'Y' block design.

To compete with the Corvette, Henry Kaiser builds a fiberglass sports car he calls 'The Kaiser-Darrin. It has V8 Cadillac overhead valve engines in them and some truly innovative improvements like sliding doors, seatbelts and a tachometer.

The big news in 1955 was that Chevrolet and Pontiac finally came out with overhead valve V8 engines.

To compete with the Corvette and Kaiser-Darrin, Ford introduces their own sports car. This all steel lightweight version was called 'The Thunderbird'. The V8 engine was available with a supercharger.

Not to be out done Studebaker builds yet another sports car, this one is called 'The Speedster". It comes with a 160 MPH speedometer and an 8,000 RPM tachometer.

I became a teenager in 1956 and life as I had known it, was about to drastically change. Previously my life consisted of my family, school, church, little league baseball, fishing, hunting and Saturday Matinees.

At the movies, I mostly loved the Westerns that today we call 'B' rated westerns or 'oaters'. Our hero's never ran out of bullets and never lost their hat in a fist fight. In the end of the picture they always got the girl but more often than not, it was his horse that he kissed before riding off into the sunset.

Now in addition to the hot rods that have been in my head for the past year or so, there were girls. Now how did they get in there? For the most part these were the same girls that I have been successfully ignoring for years.

These girls that I had known for most of my life were changing right before my very eyes. They didn't seem to giggle over nothing anymore. Their bodies were filling out with curves and bumps. They have developed hips where none had been before and their legs seemed longer. What's going on here and why do I all of a sudden want to be around them? I tell ya' it's enough to drive a fella' nuts.

At school there is an abundance of both hot rods and girls. Hot rods parked in the student parking lot and hot girls filling up the halls and class rooms.

In the school library I made a discovery one day that changed my life. In addition to the stacks of old 'Hot Rod' magazines there were many other car magazines as well. My personal favorite's been and still is, 'Car Craft' and 'Rod and Custom'.

One day in the library I found a copy of Henry Gregor Felsen's book entitled 'Hot Rod'. If you have not read it? I whole-heartedly recommend it.

As I started taking my first steps toward becoming an adult I started to broaden my horizons. I still pretty much continued to like the same things that I did as a kid, but now I was finding new things to like. My choice in music was rock n' roll and I found myself watching a lot of rock n' roll movies.

If you're not familiar with these movies let me describe some of them. In 1956 alone there were several, just to mention a few. There was 'Don't knock the Rock' starring radio disc jockey Alan Freed, Chuck Berry and Little Richard and 'Rock Around the Clock' with Wild Bill Haley and His Comets. Then there were the movies 'Rock! Rock! Rock!' which starred Tuesday Weld, Chuck Berry and Alan Freed and 'Rock Pretty Baby' with Sal

Mineo and John Saxon. Chuck Connors starred in a little known flick entitled ‘Hot Rod Girl’.

Hollywood continued making rock n’ roll movies for the next couple of years. ‘Mister Rock n’ Roll’ with Alan Freed, Little Richard and Wild Bill Haley. ‘The Girl Can’t Help It!’ starring Jane Mansfield, Fats Domino, Gene Vincent and Eddie Cochrane. ‘Go Johnny Go’ with Jimmie Clanton, Chuck Berry, The Cadillac’s and Eddie Cochrane. Last but certainly not least was, ‘High School Confidential’ starring Jerry Lee Lewis.

I liked my school, my teachers and for the first time I found myself liking the girls as much as the guys. We were quickly becoming a bunch of ‘Cool Cats’ and ‘Hipped Chicks’. Did I say hipped again? What’s happening to me.

Chapter Three

'Looking Back'

In 1956, 57 and 58, I would have been 13, 14 and 15 years old. I discovered three new fun things to do.

I started attending what was called 'sock hop dances' which were held in the National Guard Armory. It may sound kinda' lame but almost everyone that I knew went and had a great time.

Another very cool thing to do was to go to the roller skating rink. I learned to skate rather quickly and got pretty darn good at it. I remember that I loved to skate to songs like Dave 'Baby' Cortez's 'Happy Organ'.

Friends talked me into going to the bowling alley one night and I discovered that I enjoyed that as well. It took a while to learn but after a while I became a decent bowler.

Later when I started to double date, these accomplishments came in pretty handy.

The horsepower race had reached a fever pitch by 1957.

Many of Studebaker's Golden Hawk's came Equipped with Paxton superchargers and produced an unheard of 275 horses.

The 265 C.I.D. engines that Chevrolet had used in 1955 and 1956 were updated with a 283 C.I.D. engines. These engines were available with two four barrel carburetors or the newly introduced Rochester fuel injection units.

Pontiac's high powered engines sported three two barreled carburetors.

Oldsmobile's new 'J2' engine also had three two barrel carburetors and a 10 to 1 compression ratio which would produce 300 horses.

Rambler got into the race by introducing 'The Rebel' which had a 327 C.I.D. engine which would also pump out 300 horses. (Chevrolet did not produce a 327 engine until 1962 but when it did it produced 325 horses) Being lighter and faster police departments all over the country purchased the Rebel for high speed pursuit vehicles.

Plymouth brings out its secret weapon 'The Fury' with a duel four barreled carbureted 'Commando' engine. This engine at 290 horses produced 325 foot pounds of torque.

Ford puts a 312 C.I.D. interceptor engine in its Thunderbird complete with a supercharger.
Ford fans were pretty happy but sadly 1957 was the last year for the little lightweight sports car. In 1968 the Thunderbird was nearly twice as big, twice as heavy with a bigger C.I.D. engine that had a longer stroke, making it much slower at lower speeds. It became a luxury car.

In 1958 Chevrolet radically re-styled its body which was much heavier than the '57. This new body had four coil springs, instead of two in the front and leaf springs in the rear. It was available with a choice of two engines, the standard 283 C.I.D. with two or four barreled carburetors or the new big block 348 C.I.D. engine (which weighed nearly twice as much) which was available with either a four barrel carburetor or three two barrel carburetors.

The 1959 Chevrolet was even more radically re-styled than the 1958 had been. This body had horizontal tail fins and cat-eyed taillights. It had the same two engine options, neither very exciting.

In 1959, I guess that I was pretty much the quintessential sixteen year old teenager. I was in my sophomore year in high school. I was head over heels in love. With life, school, old cars, girls and rock n' roll music.

Speaking of our music, it turned out not to be a good year for rock n' roll. We were devastated to hear the news that we had lost Buddy Holly, Richie Valens and Jiles Perry 'JP' Richardson 'The Big Bopper'. They were all killed in a plane crash in an Iowa corn field.

It only got worse. Elvis Presley 'The King' of rock n' roll was still in the army and serving in Germany. Chuck Berry was in prison for violating 'The Mann Act' and Little Richard announced that he was leaving rock n' roll for the ministry. Wild Bill Haley and his Comets had left America and were touring Europe.

Thank God we still had Fats Domino, Jerry Lee Lewis, Johnny Cash, The Coasters and a few more.

!959 would go down in history as 'the year the music nearly died!'

By 1960 the horsepower race was temporarily over. Chryslers 'Hemi' was gone as were the superchargers and fuel injection units and most of the multiple carburetion systems.

The American automotive manufactures found a new fight on their hands. Small foreign cars (Volkswagen from Germany, Volvo from Sweden and MG from England) were being sold in this country and they were hurting the sales of American made vehicles.

To combat this new threat, Ford Motor Company introduced 'Falcon' a small lightweight gas efficient six cylindered engine (all the foreign cars had four cylinder engines). Falcon was available in a small truck (Ranchero), Vans and a cab over truck as well as the passenger car models.

Chevrolet built a smaller vehicle yet. It was called the 'Corvair' and its engines were rear mounted air cooled six cylinders. The Corvair was offered in passenger cars, vans and trucks.

Plymouth was marketing the 'Valiant' and Dodge was offering the 'Dart'. Both of these vehicles had front mounted water cooled six cylinders.

High school had a lot to offer guys like me. I took drivers ed. where I learn to drive and got my driver's license. I took shop class where I learned basic metal work, basic welding and some spray painting. I took auto mechanics class where I learn how to do a lot of basic repairs and maintenance.

This only fueled my desire to have and own a car of my very own. It all seemed pretty hopeless though. I didn't have a place to work on a car and I didn't have any tools. I also did not yet have the knowledge or ability to do everything that would be needed to build and have the kind of car that I wanted.

Thank God for older cousins because the few dates that I did have in my sophomore year of high school were double-dates.

Four

'Man with a plan'

Also for the first time in my life I was making money. This was my money, money that I could use for anything that I wanted to spend it on. What did I want more than anything else in the world? That's right! A car of my very own, fixed up, just the way that I wanted it.

Unfortunately every time I brought up the subject, I was told that I was too young for my own car.

Just before my junior year of high school started I took a little trip downtown and bought my own school clothes. Clothes of my choosing, clothes that I wanted to wear not clothes picked out by my parents. The rest of the money I sock away along with my dreams.

A few weeks after school started I went to visit a man who owned a small neighborhood garage. I explained to him what I had learned in school and that I knew that there was so much more to learn. Before I could continue he interrupted me by saying his garage was not a school and that he was not a teacher. He continued by saying that he had a living to make and that he was much too busy to even consider it.

I left disappointed and somewhat discouraged but I knew that tomorrow was another day. The next day I returned with a new tactic. He was kind enough to at least listen with one ear to my well thought-out proposal.

I started by saying that I understood what he had said yesterday and looking around, I said that it seemed to me that he could use someone to pick up and clean his tools. I continued with, I could sweep his floors and keep the place clean. I could even wash parts and in general be a second pairs of hands.

He considered the points that I had made and then said that he could not afford to hire an apprentice. Then he turned around and went back to work. End of discussion.

A few days later I decided to try something a little different. I aired up the tires on my bicycle and rode out to the salvage yard. I basically gave the man the same pitch telling him that I would like a job, cleaning up or pulling parts or whatever he needed done. I basically received the same answer.

I had no way of knowing it at the time but I would find out later that these two men were brother-in-laws to each other. One of them had married the other one's sister.

With the help of the school counselor I did find an after school job. Not a job that I much cottoned to but it was a job that paid a decent wage. I had been raised that if you took a job you gave a fair days work for a fair days wage.

This job was at a small neighborhood grocery store. I was the stock boy, I was the carry- out boy, and I was the clean up boy which included freezers that had not been cleaned in years. I even painted the walls inside and out.

A few weeks later the owner of the garage, stopped by to pick up some things for his wife. He spotted me right away ask and asked how I liked my new job? I told him that it was alright but not exactly what I wanted to do for the rest of my life.

A few days later, he was waiting for me when school let out. He was standing beside my bike when I got there. He introduced himself as Hank and said that he and his brother-in-law Bill, the fellow that owned the salvage yard had a proposition for me.

They had talked it over and had decided that if I was willing, they could share me. It would work like this, every other day I would work at the garage and every other day I would work at the salvage yard. Every other week it would flip-flop. Neither one was open on Sundays. It was about the same hours but it paid slightly more.

Like men we shook hands and the deal was sealed. I finished the week at the grocery store and started my new job the following Monday afternoon.

After a few days, both of the offices and shop areas were as clean as a whistle. One of the first things that I learned about the salvage yard was that it was also an auto supply. Bill tried to stock as many of the popular parts and supplies as he could afford.

I already knew the names and models of most of the cars on the road. Thanks to the library and all the time that I had spent there. Now I was learning about all the different parts, by removing, cleaning and replacing them.

At the salvage yard I was beginning to learn that many parts were interchangeable with each other.

I was living what I considered to be a dream come true. I was learning all about cars and I was getting paid too. The work was often times hard but I didn't mind one bit.

My parents were proud of me as well for showing them that I could handle all this new found responsibility. I went to school during the day and then worked three hours after that and all day Saturdays. Don't ask me how but I managed to keep my grades up as well.

I usually had a date for both Friday and Saturday nights. I was finding my way around girls just like I was cars. I found them both to be a challenging prospect.

Sundays were a day to sleep late and then catch up on family things.

My dreams of owning, building and driving my own car was, easier shared with Hank and Bill than it was with either of my parents. Being car guys themselves, they seem to understand what I was going through now and what I wanted to do in the future.

Over Christmas vacation even though business was kinda' slow, I was able to get a few extra hours.

It turned out to be a great Christmas. I for the first time was able to buy gifts for everyone in the family.

Christmas vacation ended much sooner than I would have liked. It was back to the grind, back to school, back to work, no steady girlfriend and no car.

More bad news for Rock n' Roll, Eddie Cochran (Summertime Blues) was killed in a tragic accident. He was only 21 years old and would be missed by tens of thousands of fans. He was in England with Gene Vincent and they both were in a taxi which was involved in the accident. Vincent lived but was very seriously injured and took months to recover.

Summer finally came and I thought that maybe I could work full-time. As it turned out I was given half days and Saturdays, which turned out to be great because a few days later I found my dream car.

Chapter Five
Fruits of My Labor

I knew that to buy, repair and custom build a car that I would be proud to 'tool' around in. Was going to cost a lot more money than I had so far. To make some more money I put up posters around town. These posters were to tell the world that I was available to do odd jobs. I had suspected that most of the work that I would be offered would be mowing lawns and doing yard work.

The first call that I received was from an elderly couple wanted their house painted. I made an appointment to go over the next afternoon to check it out. The house was a reasonably small wood frame house, with a single free standing garage.

The old paint was several year old and was peeling pretty bad. They asked me if I had any experience in house painting? I told them that I had helped my dad paint our house and that I had done a lot of painting at the grocery store. I told them that I would need to figure out how long it would take to scrape it and what the painting supplies would cost and I would give them a price.

I next day, after having given a lot of thought to it the night before, I went to the hardware store with a list of materials to get the cost of the paint, thinner, brushes and a scraper.

I went over to their house with what I thought was a fair price for both of us. They listened to my proposal and then thanked me saying, that living on a fixed income that it was more than they could afford. I left with all three of us a little sad.

When I got home, my mother told me that there had been another call from someone needing help. She said that the phone number was on a pad by the phone. I called the number and was told by this nice sounding lady that she had a storage shed in her backyard that was ready to fall down.

She said that she wanted it torn down. She also said that it was full of stuff, most of which she did not want or need. Five minutes later, she and I were standing in her backyard surveying the situation.

We agreed on fifty dollars to make all it all disappear. The first thing that I did was make a deal with a junk dealer that had a little store. We agreed that he would take it all. The good, the bad and the trash and he would pay me twenty-five dollars.

Once it was empty, I dismantled the shed in short order. I made two piles, the good lumber that I would save and trash that would need to be hauled off. I found a trash man who hauled it off for ten bucks.

A few days later, I was riding my bike pass the house where the old folks lived that wanted their house painted. The garage doors were opened and I couldn't believe my eyes, some kind of old car was in there.

Without giving one thought to the fact that I was trespassing, I rode up to the garage. What I discovered in there was a 1941 Ford business coupe. Business coupes came from the factory without a back seat. That space was left open, so that salesmen would have a place to put their samples and merchandise.

The car was covered in dust and it was obvious that it wasn't been driven in years. Wiping off some of the dust I could see that it was dark green. From what I could see the body was in great shape. It did not appear to have any dents or rust and the glass didn't have a crack or pock mark on it. The tire were up but were pretty badly weather cracked.

I was instantly and totally in love. I wanted this car so badly that it hurt.

I literally ran to their front door and knocked louder than I meant too. I could hear someone inside and a few seconds later the door opened. It was the man of the house, recognizing me he came outside and asks if there was something that he could do for me?

I asked him if he could tell me about the car in the garage? He motions me over to the porch swing and the two of us sit down. He told me that he had bought it brand spanking new and had driven it for over ten years.

I asked him if he had been a salesman? He smiled and said yes, that had spent most of his life on the road selling one thing or another, for one company or another. I asked him how long had it been parked in that garage? He said let's see now, I retired in 1950 and maybe drove it for another couple of years until my eyes got too bad to drive.

With my heart in my throat, I asked the million dollar question, would he consider selling it?

He looked at me for a long minute, then said that he might but it would depend on how much I was willing to offer.

Hoping to save my cash, I walked out on a climb and said you need to have your house scraped and painted and I need a car. How about this you pay for the painting supplies and I'll trade my labor for the car?

He said let me talk it over with my wife and I'll let you know. I prayed to God all the way home that he would say yes.

After two days he still had not called, so I was reasonably sure that my first proposal was not going to 'fly' I started to consider other offers and approaches that I might use. On the third day he called and asked if I could come over. Riding over there on my bike, I ran my alternative offers over in my head.

To my surprise, there on the front porch were several gallons of paint, a gallon of paint thinner and a box which contained brushes, tape, and a scraper. Once again with my heart in my throat, I knocked on the door.

When the door opened, it was the lady of the house. She said that her husband was not at home. Then she asked with a little grin, when I thought that maybe I could get started? I nearly fell all over myself saying Right Now!

I put all the supplies except for the scraper in the garage and started scraping the house. Shortly thereafter, the man of the house shows up and is pleased to see me hard at work. I ask him if he had any ladders and he tells me that he did not own a ladder, as he never needed one.

For the rest of the day I scraped what I could reach. When I got home I checked and all we had was a six foot ladder. I decided that I could make a long ladder out of some of those 2x4's that I had salvaged from the shed, that I had torn down earlier.

It took over a week to scrape the house and several more days to paint it. I thought that the place looked great and so did they. I was given the keys and title to my very own car and I couldn't have been happier.

Chapter Six

'First Fruits'

Now a labor of love was about to commence. I was ready to rebuild and re-engineer a car to my own liking.

By this time Hank and Bill had become much more than my employers, they had become friends. They had both confided in me that they were impressed with my general attitude, my work ethics and just how fast I seemed to learn.

For the past two weeks, they knew where I was and what I had been doing when I wasn't with them. Being adults they managed to contain their enthusiasm much better than I did.

The next morning, I showed both of them the title and the keys. I didn't know it but Bill had already cleared out a spot up front close to the office for me to park it while working on it.

Kidding me, Hank said ok lets go for a spin! I told them that I didn't think that it would run because it had sit for years. Hank said well let's go find out!

We took the wrecker truck over there and after some preliminary evaluations we discovered that of course the battery was junk and it had no brakes. Together we pushed it outside and Hank backed the wrecker up to it. After hooking it up we took off.

I figured that we would be headed for the garage but we were going in the wrong direction. I asked Hank where we were going? Keeping a straight face he said "we're taking her to the junk yard, that's where a crate like this belongs." Then he smiled real big and said don't worry about it!

When we got there, I was genuinely surprised at Bills generosity. After we stationed my car I asked Hank how much I owed him. He just grinned and said that he would put it on my account. Truth be known, that was one bill that never got paid.

The next day after working the morning at the garage, I headed home for a quick lunch. Then I jumped on my bike and rode out to the junk yard.

After visiting with Bill for a minute or so, he said "ya' know if she was mine I think the first thing that I would do is take the hood off, it'd be a lot easier to work on." After I got the bolts out, he helped me sit it to the side. I thank him and he headed back to his work and I went back to mine.

I already knew a lot about this model car. I knew that it had a 90 horsepower V8 flathead engine. One of the first things that the owners of this design learned was that you have to keep her cool. If she never over heated, you took the chance of warping the heads or at the least blowing one or both head gaskets. Sometimes if she got real hot you could crack her block.

Starting at the front, I removed the radiator and then sat it to the side. I would be sending it off to a radiator shop to be cleaned and then 'rodded out'. Inspecting the hoses they were soft and pretty well rotten. The fan belt had cracks in it and would also have to be replaced. I started making a list for future reference.

As I was removing the air cleaner, Hank walked up and said you're need to pull off the carburetor and fuel pump. Bring them to the garage and we'll clean out all the old gum and varnish and re-kit them. Something else you'll need to do is drain the fuel tank and then take it off so that we can clean it out as well. Oh, and blow out the fuel line. Laughing he says that oughta' keep you busy for a while.

It only took about five minutes to remove the fuel line that ran between the carburetor and the fuel pump. Three nuts and the carburetor lifted off and two more nuts to remove the fuel pump. Rapping my knuckles on the bottom of the gas tank told me that it was empty. An hour later and the tank lay on the ground. I took an air hose with a air nozzle and blew out the line.

Arriving at home I was just in time for supper. Mom had fixed my all-time favorite meal. A big pot of navy beans and ham hocks, throw in her special cornbread and you had a feast fit for a king.

I still hadn't told either of my parents that I had a car. I figured that argument could wait for some other day.

The next day being Saturday, besides working on other peoples cars we did disassemble the fuel pump and carburetor and put them in a special solution to soak. Then I went home for lunch. After lunch, I headed for the salvage yard to put in another half day.

That night I double dated with my cousin again. He had a 1950 Oldsmobile Rocket 88 with a highly worked over overhead valve V8. That car ran like a striped assed ape and he had never lost a race.

The girl that I took out that night, I had dated several times before. Her name was Sharon and she was very pretty and well put together, if you know what I mean. She liked to kiss and so did I, so that was a plus. The only negative thing was that I was beginning to think that she was about half dingy. She couldn't always remember some of the things we had done or places we had been to.

Things got a little hot at the drive-in movie and things got a little hotter afterwards. A fellow driving a 1957 Thunderbird challenged us to a drag race. A twenty dollar bit was made and the race was on. Big surprise my cousin lost. He had never lost before. We later learned that bird had a supercharger.

Speaking of surprises, the next day being Sunday a day of leisure, I went over un-announced to see Sharon. Out in the front yard were both Sharon and her twin sister Karen washing their dad's Car. It hit me like a ton of bricks, there were two of them. Now things were starting to make sense. I had been dating both of them. I liked the idea a lot but do you think that they would continue with the arrangement, NO!

Chapter Seven

'Labors of Love'

In spite of the fact that I didn't sleep real well Sunday night, Monday morning actually found me at the garage before Hank. When Hank arrived, I turned on the lights and opened the doors. Next I turned on the radio and found Jerry Lee Lewis pounding on his piano. I have converted Hank or maybe like he likes to say I perverted him into listening to rock n' roll on the shop radio. Hank didn't look too good either, so I kept the volume a few decimals lower than usual.

After giving Hank a good half days work, he showed me how to rebuild a carburetor. Taking the carburetor and fuel pump out of the cleaning solution, he had me blow the pieces dry with the air hose. He showed me the rebuilding kit which included all the necessary gaskets and needles and seats. After we finished with the carburetor we re-assembled the fuel pump. That kit also had the gaskets and a new diaphragm as well.

When we finished, I paid Hank for the new parts. I am establishing ‘a pay as I go policy’. No credit for me, I read someplace that credit makes enemies and I wanted to keep both Hank and Bill as friends. Hank says that I am wise beyond my years, I don’t know about that.

Shortly after arriving at the salvage yard, I had the carburetor installed and was starting to install the fuel pump when Bill stopped me. He says let me show you an old Indian trick. He explains to me that over time the pushrod that runs from the camshaft to the fuel pump loses a little of its length (lift) due to wear

Bill pulled the pushrod out of its hole and put it in the bench vise. Then he welded a small nut on the top of the rod and then he ground it down a little bit so that the rod is about 3/16th of an inch longer than it was.

I thanked him for the tip and his help and then installed the pump and fuel line.

Next I started inspecting the ignition system. I pulled, cleaned and re-gapped the spark plugs. Upon closer examination I decided to replace two of them. The spark plug wires had become brittle over the years so I decided to replace them. Bill said that before I bought new ones that I should check the forty model Fords out in the yard and see if there were any good ones, I did and there were several good sets.

After installing the wires I took a look at the distributor and decided to replace the points and condenser. The distributor cap and rotor look alright.

Remembering something that my grandfather had said about gasoline engines, he said that if you had air, fuel and spark you had explosion. Then if the timing was right it should run. One out of three was a good start, I had air.

She was ready for fuel, so I asked Bill if he had a gas can with some fresh gasoline? He grabbed an empty gas can and a six foot piece of garden hose and said come with me. He showed me how to siphon gas from one of the more recent wrecked cars that he had bought.

After the can was full he laughed and said now don't you be doing this at night. You might get more than gas, you might get an ass full of rock salt or worse.

I put the gas into the car and returned the empty can to Bill. I asked him if he had any good used six volt batteries? He said that he that used, reconditioned and new batteries. Then he gave me the prices. Following Bills advice I bought a reconditioned one. He said that being it was me he could warranty it like a new one.

Once the battery was installed, I told Bill that I had air, fuel and fire. I was ready to see if she would run? I gave him a quick rundown of everything that I had done and he said that he thought that I was right, it was show time.

He poured a little gas down the neck of the carburetor and said 'turn'er over'. She fired right off and ran a little before dying. We repeated the process and she died again. The third time she kept running but ran a little rough. Bill adjusted the carburetor and she smoothed right out and purred just like a kitten.

Bill said turn her off, we don't want her to get hot, remember there's no water in it.

I was as happy as a hog in mud. I settled up with Bill and headed home for supper. After a good hot home cooked meal and a little television I head off to bed. I was dog tired and I was hoping for a good night's sleep.

Life in the 1960's was promising to be a lot different than it had been in the 1950's. Lately I had been taking an interest in the six o' clock news. The top stories were the Nixon-Kennedy debates, the pill and the U.S. Supreme Court enforcing integration in the Louisiana Schools.

The next morning I headed for the salvage Yard, where I would be working. In addition to my normal duties which largely consisted of keeping the place clean, pulling parts for customers and re-organizing the parts bins. Lately Bill has been teaching me how to look up parts in the catalog rack.

For me the most interesting books were the interchange books. When dealing with used parts it's often times trial and error. Lucky for me, I have Bill who seems to know just about everything.

Chapter Eight

'So Much to Learn'

I finished my half a day and then started working on my own car. I jacked up all four corners of the car and then put jack stands under it to support it, so that it would not fall. Then I removed all four tires and wheels.

Giving the tires a good looking over, I decided that I was right the first time. The tires were not safe. I was not going to use them anyway because they were sixteen inch. Had they have been good they would have made good trade-ins, oh well.

Next I pulled all four brake drums off. The brake shoes didn't look all that bad but I had already decided to replace or rebuild everything. Brakes are certainly no place to scrimp or take shortcuts.

It doesn't matter how cool your rod looks or how fast it will go, if you can't stop the damn thing.

I totally disassembled everything down to the backing plates. Out in the shop area and out in the yard Bill has a strict 'No Smoking Policy'. So it was ok to wash parts in gasoline, as gasoline evaporates fast and cleans up easily.

Next I honed out the wheel cylinders and re-kitted them. Then I installed new brake shoes. The old brake shoes had been riveted on but the new ones were bonded on, making them much safer.

When asked Bill concurs with my thinking that the brake drums needed to be re-surfaced. Turning the drums on a lathe takes out the old grooves and gives them a much better stopping surface.

What I didn't know was that the brake shoes had to be contoured to match the brake drums, which meant that I had to un-install the brake shoes. I put the brake shoes and drums beside the radiator. The brake parts needed to go to an automotive machine shop and the radiator needed to go to the radiator shop.

The next piece of business was the 'master cylinder'. It was located under the car bolted to the left frame rail. It was a real bitch to get off. Lots of Penetrating solvent on the bolts and nuts, along with lots of muscle and sweat.

Once off, I put the cylinder in the bench vise and painstaking disassembled it, then came the honing and re-kitting just like the wheel cylinders.
That was all the time that I had for working on my car, it was time to head home for supper and a little television before going to bed.

The next morning I headed for the garage. After arriving I gave Hank a progress report. Then he said give me a hand pulling the rear axles out of the Baptist preacher's Plymouth and we'll take them and your brakes to the machine shop.

Pulling those axles turned out to be a real ordeal and I asked him if they were all that hard to pull? He said that some were easy and some were hard and some were even harder yet! The reason that we had pulled those axles, were because the bearings and seals were worn out.

The machine shop had a special press to remove and replace the worn out bearings and it was interesting to watch the process. I also watched as they turned my brake drums and contoured the shoes.

On the way back to the garage we dropped my stuff off at the salvage and Hank said that we still needed to drop my radiator off at the radiator shop, so we loaded in into the truck.

By the time we got back to the garage, we had just enough time to do a tune-up on an International truck before my shift was through.

I went home for a quick lunch and then I went to the salvage yard, where I continued with my own 'Labor of Love'. The rest of the afternoon was spent installing the brake shoes, packing the bearings with grease and installing the new grease seals. Putting the drums on and adjusting the brakes and replacing that master cylinder which went on much easier than it came off.

After supper we watched the news. The big story was about Vietnam. With Russia and Red China backing North Vietnam and France and Australia backing South Vietnam, there was lots of speculation as to whether the United States would or would not become involved?

My dad reminded me that when I did turned eighteen, that I would be required to register with the 'Selective Service'. He also said that I would be a prime candidate for the draft if America gets into the war. We like most Americans prayed that it would not come to pass.

Chapter Nine

'Loving My Job'

After a good breakfast I headed for the salvage yard. I arrived ten minutes early and the first customer of the day was already there waiting. A minute or so later Bill arrived. As Bill unlocked the door and turned on the lights, I started sweeping out the customer waiting area.

The man wanted a used starter. I checked the shelf and there was not a used one there. As bill filled the cash register with that days change, I gave the customer the prices for both a used starter and a rebuilt one.

He optioned for a used one, fifteen minutes later I had pulled and tested the starter and the man was on his way.

Bill took the opportunity to tell me that he was pleased with the way that I was making him a real good hand. I thought to myself just how proud my parents would have been to have heard it for themselves.

As they say time flies when you're having a good time because before I knew it, it was noon. I wasn't hungry so I decided to get started working on my car. The radiator wasn't back yet so I figured that 'bleeding' the brakes was the next thing that needed done.

Before I had a chance to ask if Bill could help me, a couple of guys that I knew from school stopped by to check out my car. After looking it over they seemed duly impressed, especially after I shared a few of my plans for the car.

They said that they were headed out to the old sand pit to go swimming and they wanted to know if I wanted to go with them. Overhearing the conversion Bill says that he thinks that just might be what the doctor ordered. I asked him what he meant by that and he said that all I had been doing lately was work and the car could wait another day.

When we arrived at the sand pit, I saw that most of the kids from school were there. I could hear a radio blasting out 'Willie and the Hand Jive'. Everyone was having a ball, some were swimming and some were socializing. Everywhere you looked there were beautiful girls in skimpy bikinis.

I had already dated several of those lovely creatures, so I started mingling around. I swam a little and I visited a little. By the time we decided to leave, I had dates for both Friday and Saturday nights. I arranged to double with a friend on Friday night and my cousin on Saturday night. Double dating was ok but I dreamed of the day when my car was running and I could single date.

The next day after working a half day at the garage, I rode my bike over to the new 'Burger Barn' for a cheese burger, onion rings and a milk shake. Since most of my friends knew that I had a car that I was working on, it didn't embarrass me to be seen on my bike.

After I arrived at the salvage, I visited with Bill for a minute and he told me that Hank had brought over my radiator. I bought new hoses, antifreeze and a new fan belt. After everything was installed, Bill came out and checked everything over and said that it all looked right.

Bill helped me bleed the brakes and soon she had a full solid pedal. Bill asked about the oil and filter and I confessed that I hadn't even thought about the oil. Bill checked the oil and it was full. Bill commented that the oil was dirty but that there was no water in it nor did he feel any metal shavings in the oil from the dipstick.

As the old oil was draining into a pan, Bill brought me five quarts of oil and a new oil filter. He said to take off the air filter, clean it out and put a little oil in there as well. After replacing the oil and filter, Bill said fire er' up and let's check for oil leaks and I am proud to say that there wasn't any.

Bill said that she sure 'purred' like a kitten! I was so proud. I was proud of my car and a little proud of myself too. Between working at the garage and here at the salvage and working on my own car, I felt like I was on my way to becoming a good mechanic.

The next thing that was in order was to check the grease in both the transmission and the rear end. Finding that they were both full, I took a grease gun and lubed all the fittings that I could find on the front suspension.

I told Bill everything that I had done and he thought a minute and then asked what about the steering box? Checking it I found that it was full as well but I did find another grease fitting that I had missed, it was on the clutch linkage.

It was time to put the wheels back on but I just couldn't bring myself to do it. Those sixteen's were not going back on there again, ever!

Chapter Ten

'First Custom Touch'

After several days of intense thought, I had come up with a plan, several in fact. The first plan was to use either 1949-51 Mercury passenger car wheels or Ford truck wheels. Both of these wheels were fifteen inch with a 51/2 inch bolt pattern, same as the '41. I decided that this was 'old hat' as many, many other people had done this already.

What I finally decided to do was to build my own wheels, well sort of. Out in the yard at the salvage yard, there was a fairly late model Cadillac with fifteen inch wheels complete with 820x 15 US Royal Master tires. These were the most expensive, koolest tires made at the time.

After buying the best two from Bill, I dismounted the tires and then I took the wheels and separated the outer rings from the wheel centers. Watching, Bill thought that I had totally lost my mind. Because I did the same thing with the sixteen's.

With a lot of very careful measuring, I cut down the centers of the sixteen's and laid them inside the Caddy rings. After studying this for a minute or so, Bill understood what I was going for. Bill being a much better arc welder than I would ever be took over.

Using a level, he soon had it all centered up. He tack welded it in several places and then we bolted it on the '41 to check for alignment and wobble. There wasn't any to be seen so we pull it off and Bill finished welding it. The process was repeated until both wheels were done.

After they cooled off, I prepared them for painting. I painted them 'bright red' and after they had dried, I mounted the tires back up and then I mounted them on the rear of the car.

A few days later, Bill asked me what about the front wheels? Having given this a lot of thought I said, same thing only with fourteen's. He couldn't hardly believe his ears and he asked why in the hell would you put two different size wheels on it?

I explained that I wanted to give the car a slight rake. I wanted it to be lower in the front than it was in the back. Bill just shook his head and said that the jury was out on that one.

Another look around in the yard and I found a Dodge car with two nearly new 700x14 tires mounted on fourteen inch wheels. The process was repeated and I loved the new look.

I had almost forgotten the posters that I had put up earlier. When I got home that night I found out that a man had call wanting his trees trimmed and some other yard work done. I had helped dad, do our trees and yard several times before. So I knew that we had all the necessary tools.

I had been making good money working for Hank and Bill but I had also been going through it at a pretty fast rate. The hay money and the grocery store money was mostly all gone as well. Luckily for me, that yard job led to another yard job, which led to a concrete job. I helped a man put in a new driveway.

The car was pretty much ready for its maiden voyage but it still hadn't been registered at the court house, hence no tags or insurance. I decided that it was time to tell my folks everything.

That night at the supper table, my mother slyly smiled at my dad and he said to me "how's the car coming?" I must have had the most shocked look on my face as they both burst out laughing.
Mother asked "just how long did you think that you could keep it a secret?" I was totally busted.

The next day after work, dad took me to the court house to get my tags. I never even consider sales tax, title and registration fees. Next we went to the insurance company where dad did business and got some insurance for me and the car. I was proud to be able to pay for everything and so was dad.

At this point I was damn near broke but I was the happiest guy in the world. I was also astonished at the high price of being an adult, well almost.

Chapter Eleven

'Another job well done'

Luck was really shining on me. Another man called and said that he needed help building a new garage at his home. He had heard what an excellent job that I had done helping to pour concrete on that other job. However he wasn't real pleased to find out that I could only work half days, but he said that we'd work something out.

For the next couple of weeks, I worked afternoons instead of mornings. It did not escape me what good friends that Bill and Hank had become. I appreciated them and told them so often.

I was proudly driving my car everywhere that I needed to go. I can't adequately tell you just how great it felt and how grown up I felt. Independence, mobility and freedom are some words that come close.

With the garage finished and my cash somewhat replenished. The first thing that I did was to have the '41 dueled with smithy glasspack mufflers. Man did she sound kool, you wouldn't believe the difference it made. She was starting to look and sound like a real rod.

That last month of summer, I was taking chicks out in my own car. Just me and them, another dream come true.

When school started for another year, most of the people that I knew could not believe just how much that I had matured. My folks had a hard time believing it, as did my teachers and friends. It did not come as any surprise to Hank and Bill, however.

Every day when I parked my car in the student parking lot I was so proud, proud to be among the elite of students who had their own car. So far, the '41 wasn't drawing much attention. She paled in comparison to the fender-less roadsters and the chopped and channeled couples.

In November John Fitzgerald 'Jack' Kennedy won the election and became our 35th President of these United States of America.

Some people still worried that the Catholic Church would 'woo' his decision making. Some people worried that because his father had been a bootlegger in the depression era and still had mob ties, that they could influence him as well.

November was also Thanksgiving time and the whole nation celebrated the bounties of our labors. Like most Americans we had a spread most kings would envy. I had always been a healthy eater but I almost over did it.

All too soon it was Christmas, my favorite holiday above all others. Like the year before I bought gifts for everyone including the '41. I bought her a new set of baby moon hubcaps.

The day after Christmas Hank took one look at the car and said that she looked like a Christmas tree. I was afraid that I had to agree, with her dark green body, bright red wheels and chrome hub caps she did look a little Christmassy.

I took a date to a New Years Eve party and we both drank champagne. Since I was driving I held my drinking to a minimum but my date drank quite a lot. Unfortunately, not enough to give up her most prized possession later on. Yeah you're right I am bad. The number one song in January 1961 was Del Shannon's 'Runaway' and that's just what she did.

Chapter Twelve

' New World '

Change seemed to be in the wind. It seemed to be everywhere you looked. From Greenwich Village on the east coast to San Francisco on the west coast, coffee houses were filled with 'Beatniks'.

They appeared to be deep thinking poets, dressed for the most part in black turtleneck sweaters. The males wore their hair long, goatees and dark sunglasses ruled the day and night. They recited strange sounding poetry and many played bongo drums. They were for the most part mellow drug users and just wanted to be left alone with their own kind.

The music was changing as well. Do Wop (that beautiful four and five part harmony) was losing ground to the 'Motown' sound. Rock n' roll as we had known it in the '50s was losing ground to surfing, hot rod and drag racing music.

There were all these new artists such as The Ventures with 'Pipeline', The Safaris with 'Wipe

Out', The Beach Boys with 'Surfin' Safari', 'Surfin' USA', 'Little Deuce Coupe' and 'Shut Down'. Jan and Dean with 'Surf City', 'Drag City', 'Dead Man's Curve' and 'Little Old Lady From Pasadena', Dick Dale and the Deltones with 'Grudge Run' and 'Mr. Eliminator'. The Rip Cords with 'Hey Little Cobra' and 'Three Window Couple', just to mention a few.

Two artist that I always thought should have collaborated together but didn't was Guitarist Duane Eddy. Eddy had a 'twangy' guitar 'Rebel Rouser' that would have sounded great with the greatest drummer at the time Sandy Nelson who did songs like 'Teen Beat' and 'Let There Be Drums'. It would have been so great.

All this hot rod and drag racing music was having an undesirable effect on lots of teenagers. Street racing had always been around but always on some isolated or abandoned road and always with care. Lately racing was happening in traffic and residential areas. Luckily there had been no deaths or injuries in the few accidents that had happened.

One day the Chief of Police and the Sheriff came to school to give us a good talking to at an all school assembly. The Chief spoke first and the crux of his speech was that all this drag racing on the streets had to come to a grinding screeching halt (no pun intended). I said that it was just a miracle that someone hadn't been killed and that he wanted to keep it that way.

The Sheriff whole heartedly agreed but had some good news. The sheriff told us that he had convinced the County fathers to let him convert an old section of highway that nobody used anymore into a drag strip. He told us that if we wanted this to happen, we would have to work with him and stop racing on the street!

For the most part street racing had stopped. Those that continued were caught, heavily fined and in some cases they had their cars impounded.

I knew one guy who was fined, lost his driving privileges for 30 days and his car set in the impound lot for the same 30 days. Thirty days without wheels gave a fellow something to think about.

The City, local merchants and civic organizations all chipped in and construction on the new drag strip started right away and was completed by the time school was out for the summer.

Those of us that graduated that spring conducted ourselves as adults and wanted to be treated as such and for the most part we were. Universally everyone planned to enjoy the summer before going on to college or the military or get jobs. In the mean time, most were like butterflies flying around in every which direction, experiencing life to the fullest.

I continued to work and one day after I had finished my shift, I drove out to the Dairy Barn. After ordering my food, a fellow that I had seen around who drove a tough looking fifty Mercury talked over and started a conversion.

He said that he had always liked the looks of these 41 Fords. He said that mine was looking pretty damn good but he knew how I could make it look even better! I asked him how was that? He said that he knew where one was sitting in a salvage yard that had a louvered hood. He said that it would look 'bitchin' on mine.

About that time the waitress showed up with my cheeseburger, fries and shake. My new friend told me where in a nearby town the other '41 was. After eating and a short thirty minute drive I was standing in front of the other '41.

She was a four door sedan, she didn't have any wheels or an engine but she did have the most beautiful hood that I had ever seen. Six rows of louvers. Two rows of 24, two rows of 20 and two rows of 16. It had also had been nosed (meaning the hood ornament had been removed and the holes filled). Another thing, how lucky can a fellow get it was the same color.

The owner said that she also had a Columbian two speed rear end. I had already spotted the floor shift transmission. Ford used floor shift trannys through 1939 then with the forty models, went to a column shift.

For the life of me, I couldn't figure out why someone would go to so much trouble for a four door?

Out of professional courtesy I suppose, he made me a good deal on the whole thing. A few days later, Hank and I put some wheels on the back of her and bought her to her new home, Bill's salvage yard.

A couple of weeks after, I had installed the hood. A sign painter came to town. In those days, there were 'gypsy' like sign painters that traveled from town to town. Painting signs for businesses. I hate to admit this but most were drunks. Very talented drunks, I think that it had something to do with smelling all those fumes day in and day out.

Anyway, while he was there painting a new sign for Hank. I noticed that in his truck, there were a couple of pin stripping brushes. I asked him if he did pin stripping and he said that he used to do a lot of it but hadn't done any in a while.

Man, the '41 took on a whole new personality with those wild red and white pin strips. I had been hot roddin' around a little bit. No not racing. Hell that 90 horse motor couldn't out run anything. It could hardly get out of its own way. I found out that it would peel out if you 'popped' the clutch. The clutch didn't like it at all and was beginning to slip. The adjustment was all gone as well.

Over a long weekend and with both Bill and Hanks help, we put in a new clutch and throw out bearing. While we were at it we installed the floor shift tranny and the two speed rear end. They told me to stop popping that damn clutch. So I kept it to a minimum.

The Sheriff's plan was working and everyone was happy. Everyone came out to the track. Funny thing, there was an odd by-product that drag racing had over street racing. With rigid safety inspections most rodders found out that their rods were not as safely built as they thought they were.

Once they were brought up to 'snuff' the competition was frantic.

Chapter Thirteen
'More Creativity'

The '41 was starting to attract attention everywhere I drove her and I was enjoying the feeling a lot. I thought she was so cool and so did most everyone else. I also believed that she was a work in progress and probably always would be. Some nights if I didn't have a date, I just cruised or 'tooled' around as we called it in those days.

Lately the bumpers were looking ugly to me. Truth be known, I guess that was because I had been seeing what was called 'nerf bars' on several cars. Many were featured in some of the rod and custom magazines that I had been reading.

I drew out on paper what I had in mind and went to a fabrication shop. Fabrication shops were the modern equivalent to the 'blacksmith shops' of days gone by. Now like then, these artisans would make out of metal anything that the customer wanted.

After looking at some pictures in the magazines, I shown the fabricator my drawings and specifications, he understood exactly what I wanted.

I didn't just want some cool little bumpers, I wanted something nearly as protective as the original ones. We decided to use one inch outside diameter 4130 chrome poly tubing. The new nerf bars were to be 24" long and 6" wide. We agreed on a price and I paid him in advance. Something that was ok in those days, I wouldn't dream of doing it today.

Several days later, he called and said that they were done. I went over the next day and got them, they were just what I wanted. He had done an excellent job.

A half hour later they were at the chrome shop. I had never had anything plated by them before but I had seen lots of their work.

A week or so later, Bill was welding them on and I had the only car around with nerf bars, front and rear. Again she took on a slightly different personality.

She was double tough looking on the outside but I knew something had to be done motor-wise. I also knew that she needed a new set of clothes on the inside. However, I didn't know just what to do about either.

After spending a lot of time considering just what it was that I did and did not want in a car. I came to the conclusion that the only thing that would do for me, was to have a car that looked super cool on the outside and could be used as a daily driver but was fast, very fast. That was a tall order for anyone.

Custom cars were built for car shows and were occasionally driven on special days. They were all about flawlessness. Flawlessly restyled metal work, sometimes it was hard to tell what kind of car they had been originally. Flawlessly innovative paintwork, everything from flame jobs to scallops. Everything from candy apple paint jobs to metal flake. Painter's using every color in the rainbow and then some.

Most custom cars were equipped with flawless interiors as well. Handmade seats of all kinds, many even swiveled. Interiors were done in all types of material from crushed velvet to a variety of leather styles, diamond pleats, rolled and tucked, rolled and pleated and so on.

Hot rods on the other hand mostly had but one agenda. To be as lightweight as possible and to have as high a horse powered engine as possible. To have a drive train and suspension engineered to deliver all that horse power to the asphalt.

In short, that agenda was to travel one quarter of a mile in the shortest 'E.T.' (elapsed time) as possible with the high M.P.H. as possible.

I guess that you could say that I wanted to have my cake and eat it too. I wanted a car with enough custom touches to be really cool and at the same time be brutality fast. Of course I also wanted it to be street worthy, safe and dependable. No short order.

Speaking of no short orders, I also wanted to have as much fun that summer as possible but I also wanted to do as much work as possible, so that I could make as much money as possible. Again I wanted my cake and I wanted to eat it too.

Chapter Fourteen

'Turmoil'

Summer went by much too fast. Most everybody that I had graduated with now had to decide what to do with their lives. As for me I was happy doing what I had been doing all along. I was really happy, I was happy with my life, my family and my job.

Most of the girls that I had graduated with were married or getting married or going off to college to find a husband or going off to the military to see the world.

There was one ray of sunshine however. Last year's junior girls were now senior girls and they looked better than ever. Life surely couldn't get any better than this.

Fall brought Friday night football games, cruising to the Burger Barn and then off to Lovers lane.
Whether you got lucky or not you always had fun.

With Halloween, came the first cold snap of fall and by Thanksgiving when most Americans were feeling grateful and enjoying parades, college football games on television and stuffing themselves on turkey, President Kennedy was facing controversy on several fronts.

The ‘cold war’ between the United States and the Soviet Union was heating up again. This was something that President Kennedy had inherited from President Eisenhower who had himself inherited from President Truman.

Daily the wall in Berlin, Germany was continuing to be built by the Russians. A wall separating East Berlin which was under the control of Russia, from West Berlin, which was being controlled by the United States and our allies.

This wall that was built by the easterners should have been called ‘The Wall of Shame’ because it became a blight on the landscape and a shame to the world.

Another thing America still had 50,000 of our troops in South Korea even though the war had come to an end in July 1953.

The 'Bay of Pigs' invasion into Cuba to over throw Fidel Castro was a dismal failure. The aftermath of this fiasco loomed over Kennedys head like an unrelenting black cloud.

Then he was faced with the growing problem of just what to do about the growing Vietnam turmoil.

Early 1961 left John F. Kennedy little to be thankful for. If world affairs hadn't dominated all his time, civil unrest at home surely had. The 'Freedom Riders' and the fight for 'Black Equity' was in full swing.

Christmas came right on time as it always had, Me and my family showered each other with love and gifts. We thoroughly enjoyed the season with all reverence.

New Years always seem to be a time of the renewing of all things. We were thankful for all the years before and looked forward to the New Year with both optimism and hope.

Like the rest of the world we met 1962 head on.

Long before school ended that spring, I had met, dated and started going steady with a senior girl named Kathy. Kathy was a little snip of a girl. She was five foot tall and maybe weigh a hundred pounds soak n' wet. She was a brunette and as cute as a button.

She graduated in the spring and all summer long we were almost inseparable. We went swimming at the sand pit. We went to a lot of drive-in movies and spent a lot of time at Lovers lane.

September brought the advent of the factory muscle cars and the horsepower race was on once again.

Out of the Dodge and Plymouth arsenals came the new 'Max Wedge Heads' with both 413 and 426 C.I.D. engines equipped with two Carter 650 CFM four barrel carburetors.

Ford was campaigning their new 406 C.I.D engine sporting three two barrel carburetors.

Pontiac unleashed its 421 C.I.D. engines which had a solid lifter camshaft and cast iron headers.

Chevrolet entered the race with a 409 C.I.D. big block engine with two four barrel carburetors.

For the sports car enthusiastic Studebaker markets a new fiberglass car called the 'Avanti' which had a 289 C.I.D. engine. These cars were made available with Paxton Superchargers.

For greater stopping power most of the cars were equipped with the new disc brake systems.

The music in 1962 was changing again as well. The surfing and drag racing music was quickly fading and was being replaced with mellower and more danceable music.

Chubby Checker's 'The Twist' goes all the way to number one. Joey Dee and the Starliner's 'Peppermint Twist' follows suit.

Shelley Fabres of the 'Donna Reed Show' has a number one hit on her hands, 'Johnny Angel'.
Brian Hyland sang 'Sealed with a Kiss' which resonated with all of us.

Little Eva goes crazy with 'Loco Motion'.

On a totally different note (no pun intended) a fellow hot rodder pulled up in front of the salvage yard one day. He was driving a 'T' bucket roadster and wanted to see what we had in the way of big V8s. He said that he was looking for something with more kick.

Bill showed him the biggest thing that we had in the yard. It was a 1958 Chrysler Imperial with a 345 horse 392 C.I.D. hemi. The big hemi suited him to a 'T' (again no pun intended). The only problem was that he was quite a bit short of having enough money.

In the mean time, I had been out front looking his machine over. For an engine, the T had a full race flathead with all the speed equipment that could be bought for flathead engines.

After a short conference with Bill, the other guy had bought the hemi and I had bought the flathead.

After the deal had been struck the fellow gave me a complete run down on his old 'mill' as he called it. It was a 1948 Mercury 239 C.I.D. engine that had been 'ported and relieved'. Up on top was one of

Vic Edelbrock's aluminum intake manifolds complete with three two barrel Stromberg carburetors activated by progressive leakage.

On either side of the intake manifold were two Offenhauser aluminum finned high compression heads. Below the heads were a pair of Fenton cast iron headers. Inside the engine was a ¾ race Iskenderian racing cam.

The ignition was handled by a Harmon-Collins duel coil set up with duel points.

The engine had chrome accessories all over it and it was so cool that it almost hurt your eyes to look at it. The engine screamed classic hot rod, but as I later learned the engine in our family station wagon had both more cubic inches and more horse power.

Bill bought my old engine but would have to wait until the swap was made to get it. In retrospect after selling the old engine to Bill, the new one was fairly cheap.

Chapter Fifteen
'Life Changes'

It seemed like before I could blink an eye I was a married man. We had a lovely small formal Church wedding. We were surrounded by our families and friends. Hank and Bill were both our 'Best Men'.

We set up housekeeping in a rented house and I discovered that married life didn't come with as many changes as I had thought that it would.

We were both working which really helped with the finances. For the first time I found myself doing things like grocery shopping. We were living together but it still felt like we were still going steady. We still went to a lot of movies and did the things that we had always done.

One Sunday afternoon I pulled into the gas station where I normally buy my gas and I saw the strangest thing. Standing around a 1957 Ford retractable hardtop were several people. The top which normally folded up and disappeared into the trunk was stuck, straight up. It would not go on up and it would not go down, no matter what anyone tried.

Ford built these cars for three years 1957, 58 and 59. They were designed to give the owners two cars in one, a two door hardtop and a convertible.

Speaking of owners, it didn't take long to figure out that two of the couples standing around, came with the car.

To add insult to injury, one of the guys that had been watching said that he knew some other folks that this had happened to and it cost a small fortune to get it fixed.

The owner's wife asked her husband what are we going to do? He answered I don't know! We certainly can't drive it home like this! I asked how far are we talking about? The husband said a little over three hundred miles.

I explain to them that I worked at the only garage around and that if anyone short of the Ford house that could fix it, it would be Hank. I left to go find him but he was no where around, neither was Bill. I could only guess that they had gone somewhere together.

I went back to the station and explained the situation. The man shook his head and said that somehow the four of them had to be back at work in the morning.

A light bulb went off in my head and I excused myself again and drove over to a friend of mine that sold used cars. Luckily he was home and in a few minutes I knew what the car would sell for if the top worked and what it was probably worth as is.

On the way back I stopped at the bus station for ticket prices and departure times. When I arrived back at the station, I had a loosely put together plan.
I told them that I only saw two options for them to consider. First I told them what four bus tickets would cost and the departure times. I said you could take the bus home and tomorrow I would see about getting their car repaired.

The husband asked me what was option number two? I told him that I would buy it from him for x numbers of dollars. He screamed like I had struck him with a knife. That ain't half of what the car is worth!

Between them, they had enough money for two tickets. All four worked and all four needed to go home. After a huddle conversation the husband came over and said ok, but he would have to mail me the title.

I went home for the money. This was money that we had been saving for a down payment on a home of our own. I drove back over and paid the man. Then I took them to the bus station two at a time.

I was feeling a little guilty, so I said "tell you what, the bus doesn't leave for another hour. I'll throw in a free meal."

The next day after looking her over, Hank called the Ford house and they told him what all to look for. She had hydraulic pumps which were activated by a series of solenoids and switches. As I recall it didn't take a whole lot to fix her.

Kathy and I drove that car for a long time and you can believe me when I tell you that every time we put the top down, we wondered if this was the time she'd stick again. Even with that being said, where's nothing like spending the summer in a convertible.

When you're young and in love, it is a wonderful state to be in and all seemed right with the world.

Having a second car gave me the time to change out the engine in the '41 at an unhurried pace. She had always been fun and cool to drive, now more so than ever.

Chapter Sixteen
'A Troubled World'

In October, like the rest of the world we here in America were shook wide awake by the 'Cuban Missile Crisis'. For thirteen days it looked like maybe we might be thrown into a war with Russia, but cooler heads prevailed and the disaster was avoided.

By December 31st, America had 11,300 soldiers in South Vietnam supposedly serving as 'military advisors'.

It seemed to most Americans that between Russia, Cuba, Red China and North Vietnam that we were almost destined to go to war with someone. Many feared that this would be the beginning of another World War.

Kathy's mother and mine as well, feared that even being married that I could be drafted if this came to pass. Nobody that I personally knew wanted us to become involved in another war.

Both my father and my new father-in-law knew that if I should become drafted that I would proudly serve my country. On the same token they both advised me against enlisting.

Early in 1963 the music suddenly took off in several different directions.

On January 11th the first American discotheque opened in Los Angeles, California. It was called 'The Whiskey-A-Go-Go'. We all wondered just what was 'Disco Music' anyway. As time went on we were to find out that it was not for most of us.

February signaled the beginning of the British Invasion bringing us something called 'Beatle Mania'. Universally it was loved by most everybody.

The beatnik generation that most people hadn't fully understood or appreciated was now fathering an even bigger movement of 'Flower Children' that called themselves 'Hippies'.

These hippies which seemed to be everywhere were fueled by a new radical musical genre 'drug induced psychedelic music'. This movement advocated love, peace and tranquility. I don't know whether it was the drugs or the tranquility that created all the 'free love' in young women but everyone hippie or not got in line for it.

About this same time a woman by the name of Betty Friedan wrote a book entitled 'The Feminine Mystique'. This book created a fever pitch within multitudes of women. This book started yet another movement banding women of all ages and walks of life together.

This movement which most men did not understand incited women everywhere to burn all their bras. This new feeling of freedom in women was enthusiastically embraced by men as the most wonderful thing to come down the pike in like forever.

George Wallace became the Governor of Alabama vowing 'segregation forever' in his state.

This action and others like it created the now famous 'March on Washington'. Where a quarter of a million people gathered together to hear Martin Luther King's 'I Have a Dream' speech.

This leads to a march from Selma, Alabama to Montgomery. Race riots broke out in Birmingham resulting in a violent altercation between the police and the protesting demonstrators.

On the home front, that summer we raced the '41 at the drag races nearly every Saturday. The class that they put us in, we were able to win most of the races and the trophies were stacking up.

In the 'dragster' classes where was only one flathead powered dragster running at our strip. It belonged to a fellow named Ron. Ron was physically too big to drive it and he was having disagreements with the guy that he had driving it.

One day after a particularly bad argument the driver had had enough and quit. To cool off Ron walked around the pits for a while looking at all the other cars. While looking at the '41 we talked flatheads and he asked me if I would like to try his dragster on for size?

I had never driven a dragster before but I had thought from time to time about possibly building one. I kinda' figured that if you could drive, you could drive anything. If you had an ear for engines and knew when to shift gears and knew how to nurse out of an engine whatever she had to give, you were a driver. So I said yeah that I would give it a try.

You may already know that dragsters like everything else on the track are divided into classes.
There are gas classes and fuel classes. There are blown (superchargers) and un-blown classes. Then they are broke down into classes determined by their cubic inch displacement.

The flathead dragster was in the F/GD class. It was carbureted un-blown running on gasoline. Ron's dragster's main competition was powered by a highly modified GMC six cylinder engine with a 'Wayne' head and multiple carburetors

The flathead had never beaten the GMC and that was the heart of the rub!

I took it out for a couple of time trials. The first time I didn't lean on it too hard as I mostly wanted to get a feel for it. It tracked real well and had a good feel to it. The second time I opened her up pretty good and then I felt like I was really for the real thing.

When it came time for open competition, I would have like to run against one of the dragsters that Ron normally won against but it was not be. First crack out of the bag we were up against the GMC.

We pumped up the fuel pressure and gave her a push, she fired right up. In the staging area I lit her up a little. Once staged I watched the Christmas tree light up and as soon as the green light lit I dropped the hammer on her.

The adrenaline rush as I emerged out of the smoke was totally unreal and it was like I was on automatic pilot. The race was so close that I thought that it was a tie. Later I learned the light actually went off on our side first.

My fate was sealed. Ron said that I was a natural and he was unbelievably happy. It had been a great day all around. The '41 had also won its class.

Ron and his wife Patty insisted on taking Kathy and I out to eat. Over T Bone steaks, Ron told us about his plans to build a new dragster. The new dragster would be a sleeker, longer and much faster. It would be powered by a small block V8 Chevrolet engine and would run on nitro methane fuel.

As Kathy was holding her breath I told Ron that I didn't think that I was the man to pilot that. As Kathy was exhaling Ron said that maybe I was right.

Ron and I made a deal for me to finish the season and then we'd see what was what. We raced on several different tracks with Ron paying all the bills.

I only lost one race that whole season and that had been caused by a mechanical failure. An axle had snapped and we lost a wheel. It didn't bother me much but it scared the hell out of Kathy.

As the season was coming to a close and Ron had already started building the new dragster, I asked him if he would sell me the old one? He said drive the Chevy for me and I'll give you the flathead!

Chapter Seventeen

'Unbelievable Tragedy Strikes'

On November 22nd, just six days before the nation was to sat down at its dinner tables and enjoy another Thanksgiving dinner, tragedy struck. Someone or rather a group of some ones literally sucked the life blood out of the American people by assassinating our President. The President of the United States of America was shot to death in Dallas, Texas.

The loss of John F. kennedy was felt by everyone for many years to come. Each of us privately wondered if they could kill the President, just how safe were any of us?

Christmas 1963 was a somber bittersweet time, but as they say life goes on. I recently saw a friend's home movie of that Christmas and was reminded of several things that I guess I had just forgotten.

Blond furniture was all the rage and most of us had entertainment centers in our homes the size of 'coffins', in our living rooms.

There's something else that I'll bet that you have forgotten because I had, silver aluminum Christmas trees with red, blue, green and orange color wheels.

Watching the children opening their gifts I was reminded once again of 'Chatty Cathy' dolls, 'Mr. Mercury Robots' and 'metal toy cash registers.

January brought us another new year filled with new music and renewed hopes.

'The Animals' gave us 'The House of the Rising Sun'. Many people thought that it might very well be America's theme song for the Vietnam era.

Even though 'The Beach Boys' had four hits that year they were steadily losing ground to the British. First with 'The Dave Clark Five' which was touring America and 'The Beetles' which had no less than a dozen hits that year.

'Chuck Berry' gave us a much needed new cruising song with 'No Particular Place to go'. Which was really kind of poetic because most of us didn't have a clue, as to where we were going anyway.

Sam Cooke gave us one more hit song before being gunned down and killed by the manager of 'The Hacienda Hotel' in Los Angeles.

The Ford Motor Company designed and released the most innovative car since the little Thunderbird. This new car was called 'The Mustang' and was the only car ever to receive the coveted 'Tiffany Award' for excellence in American design.
The Mustang sold for an incredibly low price of $2,350 for a couple and $2,695 for a convertible. Within weeks all available stock had been sold and long waiting list had been created.

Like most career politicians, Lyndon Baines Johnson had dreamed of someday becoming the President of these United States. The reality of it came so fast and so un-expectantly that he was even more at a loss, as what to do about America's vast problems than President Kennedy had been.

'The Civil Rights Act of 1964' prohibited ethic discrimination which not only included employment opportunities but the military draft as well.

While it may be true that 'draftees' were a minority of the total number of America's armed forces, over 80% of these draftees became infantry riflemen. Infantry riflemen accounted to slightly over one half of our casualties.

The Vietnam War unlike any war that we had ever been involved in was disliked by most everyone.

A draft resistance movement was supported by not only those that you would expect (students, pacifists and clergy) but civil rights and feminists organizations, Veterans of World War Two and Korea, as well.

There were massive demonstrations, draft card burnings and protests at induction centers and draft boards.

Never the less from 1964 to 1975 there were 2,215,000 young men drafted.

Being married with a child on the way I was never drafted. For me this has always been a two sided coin. On one side, after hearing all the horror stories from my friends that did somehow survive, I have always felt extremely grateful that I didn't have to go.

The other side of that coin, I have always felt a certain amount of guilt for not having gone.

Throughout the years there is something else that I have always felt. We each of us owe a debt to all of those that did go that we can never repay. I also think that it is utterly deplorable the way we (America) has treated these returning warriors. They have been treated like we are ashamed of them and what we made them do on our behalf. They fought to defend this Country's honor with their blood, sweat and tears with all honor.

Reader; If you are one of these warriors " THANK YOU" FOR YOUR SERVICE AND YOUR LIFE!!!!

Chapter Eighteen

'In the Name of Art'

I woke up the next morning asking myself a question that had been asked by countless others for centuries.

Does art imitate life or does life imitate art?

If you define 'art' as the written word in the form of books, magazines and the visual world of electronic devices such as tablets, computers, television and theatrical performances both live and recorded. Then the answer to both questions must unequivocally be 'yes'.

Life imitates or influences art as seen through the eyes of the artist. Which often times can be dishonest, distorted or just plain inaccurate. Then that happens the lives of the consumer can in some cases become corrupted, changed or altered.

The reason that I'm giving you this social and media lesson is because most of us can read a book or magazine, watch a movie for its educational or entertainment content and understand that it was created for that very purpose.

There are people among us let's say ten percent or more that have a real problem distinguishing reality from fantasy. Their very lives can be influenced to one degree or another, especially if that was the primary intent of the artist. That in its self may not be a good or healthy thing.

Bear with me because I am about to tie a ribbon around this whole thought.

There have always been rebellious people, especially impressionable teenagers. Within the growing process of each of us there is this natural seeking of knowledge and wisdom. Some of us if not all of us can be led astray by misinformation and exploitation.

Let's look at a few seemingly innocent art works that had devastating effects on the over impressionable.

In 1953 Marlon Brando starred in a motorcycle gang movie entitled 'The Wild One'. The movie was exciting and entertaining to most people who saw it. Many others were so moved that they went out and bought a motorcycle and found a gang to join or started one of their own.

I've been told that they were attempting to find something in their lives that was missing. My guess is that damn few if any found it.

In 1955 James Dean starred in a drama about emotionally confused suburban middle classed teenagers called 'Rebel without a Cause'. This movie created in some a need to be heard, a need to be understood. The end result was somewhat the same.

Art imitating life or life imitating art, whichever a few months later Dean who had everything to live for was killed in a high speed car crash.

In 1956 John Cassavettes and Sal Mineo starred in a movie entitled 'Crime in the Streets'. A big city street gang called 'The Hornets'. Without direction the Hornets ran amuck looking for trouble and their own brand of justice.

The movie creates street gangs popping up where none had been before.

From the subjective to the utterly ridiculous in 1968, Christopher Jones starred in a movie entitled 'Wild in the Streets'. In this drug induced fantasy Jones portrays a 22 year old millionaire singing idol who is elected President of the United States. After fourteen year olds get the vote, everyone over the age of thirty are put into 'Paradise Camps' to live happily ever after on LSD.

As near as I can tell this had absolutely no effect on society what so ever other than to escalate the already growing drug use among young people.

Also in 1968 Hunter S. Thompson wrote a shocking expose 'Hells Angels: the Strange and Terrible Saga of the Outlaw Motorcycle Gang'.

Thompson infiltrated the gang and lived their lifestyle for several months. After the book was published it was rumor that the gang made several unsuccessful attempts on his life. Like the Marlon Brando movie this caused many more to join the lifestyle.

A year later in 1969 The Harley Davidson Motorcycle Company received a much needed shot in the arm. Michael Parks starred in a television series entitled 'Then Came Bronson'. The series was based on the true life adventures of motorcyclist and stuntman Bud Ekins.

Parks rides around on a Harley Davidson 'Sportster' getting into one misadventure after another.

Harley Davidson sells sky rocket all over the country and soon stock is depleted and a huge waiting list is created.

Then the largest American cult film ever was produced. Peter Fonda and Dennis Hopper hit the screen and road with the epic movie 'Easy Rider'.

Chapter Nineteen

'Age of Aquarius'

Also in 1969 a half a million of America's young people showed up on Max Yasqur's 600 acre dairy farm outside Bethel, New York. This farm was located some 43 miles from Woodstock, New York. This gathering was advertized as 'The Woodstock Music Festival'.

This was sub billed as 'An Aquarian Exposition' Three days of peace and music. Bob Dylan who made his home near Woodstock and Credence Clearwater Revival were some of the first acts to sign up. As it turned out Dylan was unable to attend.

As it started coming together many performers and groups jumped on the bandwagon. Just to mention a few there was Arlo Guthrie, Janis Joplin, Sly and the Family Stone, The Who, Jefferson Airplane, The Grateful Dead and a very pregnant Joan Baez.

The festival was closed on Sunday by Jimi Hendrix. Among the groups that were invited to perform and did not make it for whatever reason was Jim Morrison and the Doors.

Unbelievable to me is that there were only two recorded fatalities that whole weekend. One was a heroin over dose and the other one happened, when a neighboring farmer ran over a sleeping attendee with a tractor and plow.

There were also two recorded births, so I guess all and all things kinda' balanced out.

In October 1970, twenty seven year old Janis Joplin, the undisputed queen of Psychedelic soul music was found dead from a heroin and alcohol over dose.

A month later twenty eight year old Jimi Hendrix was found dead of a drug over dose. It was said both before and after Hendrix's death that he was the single greatest electric guitarist that ever lived. Being a Stevie Ray Vaughn fan, I have to wonder. I have seen Vaughn dozens of times in person and only seen Hendrix on tape. They both were great.

Did you know that Hendrix was an enormous 'Little Richard' Fan? He was once quoted as saying that he wanted to do with his guitar what Little Richard did with his voice.

A short ten months later in July of '71, twenty sever year old Jim Morrison was found dead in Paris, France of a drug and alcohol over dose. Morrison was both a prolific poet and songwriter. His musical style was a expansion of his two idols Elvis Presley and Frank Sinatra.

I find myself needing to apologize to you the reader. In my enthusiasm of the moment I have gotten way ahead of the story that I was writing for you! Again I profoundly apologize. Now where was I? Oh yeah!
I believe that we were back in 1964. Johnson was President and our everyday world was filled with tension, turmoil and pain! Not all that different than today.

Ok let's go to something a little more pleasant to think about.

Drive-in theatres were still going strong. For the kids we had 'Mary Poppins' and 'Lady and the Tramp'. For us adults we had 'My Fair Lady', 'Gold Finger' and 'From Russia with Love'. Some of my personal favorites were ‘Dr. Strangelove’, ‘A Fist Full of Dollars’, ‘Cheyenne Autumn’ and of course John Wayne’s ‘Circus World’.

I did a lot of drag racing that summer. True to his word, Ron gave me the flathead dragster. I must admit that the first few times behind the wheel of a very powerful nitro and alcohol guzzler scared the living hell out of me. I never let Ron or Kathy see it though.

I think being scared (a lot at first and then a little later on) made me a safer and better driver. I don’t give a damn what anybody else tells you, getting cocky and overly confident will get you killed or seriously injured.

Something else that I’m neither proud of nor ashamed of, is that I lost the first half a dozen races. Ron didn’t know what to expect of me or the new dragster, but he was patient.

After the dragster and I got better acquainted we started to win our share of the races that we had. As I started to push the envelope we started to find all those little things that needed to be fine tuned.

We were going faster and faster with lower and lower E.T.'s.

Chapter Twenty

'Bittersweet Times'

I took Kathy to see a new movie starring Frankie Avalon and Annette Funicello. The movie was entitled 'Bikini Beach'. It was a light headed, I mean light hearted movie about our generation. It contained Rock n' Roll music, hot rods, surfing and a comical motorcycle gang.

A year or so later the gang was back with a different film. It was more of the same but with a drag racing theme. We enjoyed the film immensely.

All too soon summer was coming to an end and fall would soon close in around us.

Winter always brought our favorite holidays Thanksgiving Day, Christmas and a much need New Years Day. We were surrounded by family, friends, gifts and good food, the truly important things of life. Not the least of which, was the never ending hope of a better future and world.

In 1965, Mitch Ryder and the Detroit Wheels hit the music scene with an enjoyable sound that had been sorely missed by our generation, old time rock n' roll. This group desperately tried its best to return the music back to the happy days of the 1950's.

They had several hit songs like 'Jenny Take a Ride', 'Devil with the Blue Dress on' and 'Sock it to Me Baby'. The care free and happy days were short lived however as things started to heat up and got down right 'hot'.

By March President Johnson had sent another 50,000 troops into South Vietnam. That same month the draft boards across this great nation drafted another 35,000 of our youngest and brightest.

Speaking of heat, that summer was a scorcher but the really hot spot was Los Angeles, California with the rioting that took place in 'Watts'. The Watts Riot as it would become known lasted for five days and nights. Looting, burning and lawlessness ruled the time.

When it ended thirty four were dead with another 1,032 people injured. There were nearly 3,500 people arrested and there was over $40,000,000 that's right, forty million dollars worth of damage.

The news on television reported that when it was finally over, the streets of Watts resembled an all out war zone in some far away foreign country. It bore no resemblance of its former self. It was totally unbelievable that this could possibly have happened to an American city.

In the midst all of this tragedy life went on for most of America.

On August 15th , the last day of the Watts riot, 3,000 miles away in New York City 'The Beetles' performed live at Shea Stadium in front of 55,600 screaming fans. This was the first of the stadium concert performances to be given by the Beetles.

In September 'Sandy Koufax' pitches a perfect game against the 'Chicago Cubs'. Between pitchers Sandy Koufax and Don Drysdale, the Dodgers won the World Series against the 'Minnesota Twins', four games to three.

1965 became a pivotal point in my drag racing career. I could not fault Ron in any way for his desire to want to go even bigger and better. The small block Chevrolet engine was replaced by a big block Chevrolet engine. Its new engine was not only injected but became blown as well.

The season did not start well at all. With the 'normal' problems associated with a new rail job, we had two minor crashes. The first one was just simply too much horsepower and torque for the chassis.

Once that was corrected the second one was the result of a bad fuel mixture creating a fire. Through the Grace of God I was not burned.

By mid-season, I had seen the handwriting on the wall as they say. Ron respected my decision to quit and we remained good friends. As Clint Eastwood once said in one of his many movies, "a man has to know his limitations!" I had reached and understood mine.

For me that aspect of drag racing had ceased to be fun. It had become dangerous, not exciting as it had once been. I truly hope that you can see and appreciate the difference.

I still had within me the love of the sport. I was just scaling it way back. I continued racing the flathead and the enjoyment of doing so brought me great joy.

I must admit however that I wanted to now build a faster rail. I toyed with the idea of building a twin engine dragster. I could use both flat heads, It was way past time that the ’41 should get a new heart transplant.

Chapter Twenty one

'Searching For Good News'

The evening news continued to bring us nothing but bad news.

On November 2nd Norman Morrison (no relation to Jim Morrison of the Doors fame) commits suicide in front of Secretary of Defense Robert McNamara's office in Washington D.C. by dousing himself with gasoline and setting himself a blaze.

One week later on November 9th, Roger Allen LaPorte set himself on fire and burns to death in front of the United Nations building in New York City.

By the end of the year there were 400,000 American soldiers in Vietnam. This results in massive protests and demonstrations from San Francisco to London, England.

Throughout 1966 the war in Vietnam escalated as did the protests and demonstrations.

Just as large as these anti war demonstrations were, so were the civil rights demonstrations.

Originally black American wanted to achieve equality through peaceful means. Martin Luther King Jr's approach was totally different than Malcolm X's. Malcolm X advocated violence and promoted the concept of fighting fire with fire. His particular hatred was aimed at all white supremacist of might and there was no shortage.

The American Nazi Party which had been founded in 1960 had a common bond with other groups of haters, such as the Ku Klux Klan. These groups not only hated blacks but also anyone that was different such as the Jews, etc!

Malcolm X was assassinated in February 1965.

On the heels of Sam Bower's (the KKK's Grand Wizard) conviction for the murder of Vernon Dahmer (the President of Forest County's NAACP in Hattiesburg, Mississippi) by firebombing his home. There was a newly formed black hate group called 'The Black Panthers'.

Even though these things dominated the evening news there were other news related commentaries.

The clothing fashion world was temporarily going crazy over the influence that the 'Carnaby Street' designers and manufactures of London, England had over the new 'must have' designs. For the most part many of these designs were just outrageous and sometimes even weird.

Giving credit where credit is due, they did give us the miniskirt and hot pants. So I guess that it wasn't all bad.

Our television sets went color and for the first time we saw color programming, everything from 'The Oscars' to the 'Miss America Pageant.' By the way Deborah Bryant of Overland, Kansas was crowned that year.

Other television shows that you may remember premiered that year. The biggest being 'Star trek', following closely behind were 'Batman' and 'The Green Hornet'.

On the evening news for the first time we got to see the war in Vietnam in red, white and blood.

Russia may have landed on the moon first but we built the Houston Astrodome, the biggest building of its kind anywhere to have ever been built.

Musically Simon and Garfunkel gave us 'Sounds of Silence' and the Rolling Stone contributed to the cause with 'Paint it Black'. There were other new voices to be heard such as 'The Mamas and the Papas', 'The Monkeys', Jefferson Airplane' and 'Buffalo Springfield'.

Hank, Bill, and I formed a three way partnership. Each of us now owned a one third interest in both businesses. I certainly hoped that this partnership would be successful not just for the obvious reasons but mainly because I had talked both of them into it.

It was agreed among all three of us that he money that I was investing would be used to update and improve the businesses. I was now a full time business man, a full time husband and father and part time drag racer.

Don't ask me how I found the time to do all three but I did. Truth be known, I don't know myself.

I yanked the engine out of the dragster and totally disassembled it. Then I yanked the engine out of the '41. After making them as identical was possible, I replaced the intake manifolds. The '41 had three two barrel carburetors where the dragster had four two barrel carburetors.

Both engines now sported Edelbrock single four barrel manifold with the largest Holley carburetors that I could find. Next after weeks of searching I found and purchased two Paxton superchargers.

The old frame was not long enough or strong enough to support two engines. So a new one had to be built and she got a new rear end. The rear end came out of a wrecked GTO that I had bought and was a posi-trac. We changed the ring and pinion gears to one much lower gear and shortened the axles.

The rear wheels were bigger with bigger racing slicks. I toyed with the idea of trading the American 10 spoke front wheels for spooled 40 spoke wire wheels but in the end I thought better of it.

After some cosmetic work she was ready to paint, once that was completed there was a sign on the front cowling that read 'Flatheads Forever'.

The '41 had sat for quite some time and I decided that it was time to put her back into commission. I wanted to put the 389 C.I.D. engine with the three two barreled factory carburetion system out of the GTO in her.

The first problem I saw was that, the Columbia two speed rear end wouldn't work with anything but a flathead. I removed and replaced it with an open drive line rear end out of an Oldsmobile 88. This rear end has two leaf springs instead of the single transverse spring. It took all the engineering that we all had to get the job done.

The engine and four speed transmission fit in there without too much cutting and a custom driveshaft had to be made. The clutch linkage was handled with a hydraulic cylinder. All together I have to say that it was a lot harder than I thought that it would be.

By summer both the ’41 and the dragster were ready and I was itching to go. I only ran the ’41 a few times, mostly because I was curious as to what she would do. She could have held her own and won most of the races. She was never really a race car or she still wasn’t.

The rail initially had a few bugs as you might well imagine. Soon enough she was turning heads and was turning in quite impressive E.T.’s (Elapsed time).

Ron was both impressed and pleased with the new flathead rail. He said that he couldn’t have done a better job himself. I doubted what he said was true but I accepted the compliment with both pride and honor.

Chapter Twenty Two

'Broadening My Horizons'

A few months later, a gentlemen from our local 'Rotary Club' stopped by the garage to visit with us, he was recruiting new members. After giving us he sales pitch we decided that our company could do worse than to belong to 'Rotary International'.

Hank and Bill decided that since I was the scholarly one of the outfit that I should be the one to attend the weekly meetings.

Membership in the club included local business men as well as the county judge, the high school principal and the superintendent of school.

The winter of 1966 had come and gone bringing a beautifully green spring. Summer brought another year of swimming in the old sand pit, drive-in movies and lots of drag racing.

1967 started out very much like the year before. There was more war with more troops deployed. There were more protests like the one at Kezar

Stadium in San Francisco where over 40,000 attended.

Muhammad Ali (Cassius Clay Jr.) was stripped of his World Championship title for refusing to be inducted into the U.S. Army.

Years later he would be allowed to return to the world of professional boxing, where he once again became the Champion. Until his death in 2016 he was known by the whole world as 'The Greatest'.

Getting back to 1967, the inner cities of America exploded with wide spread rioting, burning and looting in Cleveland, Newark and Detroit.

The worst of these being Detroit, where on July 23rd some 7,000 National Guard Troops were brought in to restore peace and to bring back law and order to these lawless streets.

1967 can be remembered for lots of other things such as 'Twiggy' (the super skinny model) and clothes made of paper which even included miniskirts, believe it or not.

The Beatles continue to reign supreme in the music world with their new release 'Sgt. Pepper's Lonely Hearts Club Band'.

This was also the summer of 'Love-ins'. When many young American were notoriously promiscuous, they smoked a lot of dope and grooved to the music of 'The Grateful Dead', 'Jefferson Airplane' and 'The Byrds'.
At the movies, we watched and enjoyed 'The Graduate', 'Bonnie and Clyde', 'The Dirty Dozen', 'To Sir with Love' and my personal favorite 'Cool Hand Luke'.

On television, we watched 'The Fugitive', 'The Beverly Hillbillies', 'Peyton Place' and 'I Dream of Jennie'.

I recently heard someone on television comment that in 1967, gasoline was 33 cents a gallon, the average price of a movie ticket was $1.25 and that the Federal Minimum Wage had just gone to $1.40 per hour.

The new giant 23" color television set cost $489, if you had a good job let's say $75 a week it would take over six weeks to pay for it, if you didn't spend a nickel on anything else. Even with that said lots of America households had one.

All of a sudden automotive safety becomes a very big deal. The National Transportation Safety Board is created on the heels of The National Traffic and Motor Act and the implementing of The United States Department of Transportation (DOT).

We all owe Ralph Nader a huge debt of gratitude for taking on the American automobile manufacturers. All or most of this new legislation was brought about because of a book that he wrote which was entitled 'Unsafe at any speed'. Nader appeared before congress numerous times on our behalf, the America people.

General Motors President James Roche and the heads of the other auto manufacturers were forced to appear before The United States Senate to answer questions on many of these issues.

The very first 'Super Bowl' was played at the Memorial Coliseum in Los Angeles, California. The Green Bay Packers won over The Kansas City Chiefs, the score was 35 to 10.

Jimmie Hoffa started serving an eight year sentence for fraud and jury tampering.

Evil Knievel jumped his motorcycle over 16 cars lined up end to end but failed to jump over 'The Fountains of Caesar's Palace' in Las Vegas. Nevada.

The King Elvis Presley took Priscilla for his bride, while enjoying a new contract with RCA.

Singer Otis Reading dies in a plane crash. He was only twenty-six years old.

Some fairly new musical groups now being enjoyed included David Jones who billed himself as David Bowie, a name that he borrowed from his hero Jim Bowie who died at The Alamo in San Antonio, Texas in 1836.

Others included Moody Blues, Pink Floyd and The Bee gees.

The big Christmas gift for men that year were Electric Shavers which sold for around $16.00. The big Christmas gifts for the ladies included Electric Hair Roller Sets and Portable Facial Bath Stations, each costing around $30.00.

Boys enjoyed getting HO Scale Race Tracks, Walkie Talkies and Binoculars. Girls were given Barbie Dolls, Barbie Doll Houses and Cinderella Pumpkin Carriages.

Chapter Twenty Three

'Even More Changes'

In March of 1968 we celebrated my twenty-fifth Birthday, I wondered could I really be that old?

All too soon this great nation was engulfed in sadness once again.

On April 4th civil rights champion Martin Luther King Jr. was assassinated. Dr. King's assassination sparked off mass riots in cities all across the north. The hardest hit were Baltimore, Boston, Chicago, Detroit, Kansas City, Newark and in Washington D.C.

Three months later on the eve of the California primary election, Presidential hopeful Robert Kennedy was assassinated.

I had to wonder at the time, between the war, the riots and the protests and the assassinations, just how much more could America and her people endure.

In July Abbie Hoffman, Jerry Rubin and Paul Krassner start the 'Yippee Movement'. Large numbers of these yippees demonstrated on the floor of The New York Stock Exchange. They also demonstrated off and on for six weeks during the Chicago Democratic National Convention.

Richard Nixon once again ran for the Presidency of the United States on the Republican ticket.

President Johnson decided not to seek re-election. The Democratic Party decided to run Hubert Humprey.

Democratic Governor George Wallace decided to run as an independent, is was largely supported by the Deep South.

In the mean time former first lady Jacqueline Kennedy married greek shipping magnate Aristotle Onassis.

In the November elections, Nixon won the Presidency with 43.4 % of the votes. Humprey got 42.7 % and Wallace barely managed 13.5 % which was far lower than most Americans feared.

That summer I cut back on the racing and did more family things.

On July 20th American Astronaut Neil Armstrong became the first man to walk on the surface of the Moon. Armstrong spoke these immortal words “that is one small step for man and one giant step for mankind”.

Earlier I fairly well covered Woodstock and the subsequent deaths of Joplin, Hendrix and Morrison and have no desire to return there, so moving on……

Western Movies were once again big that year with ‘Butch Cassidy and the Sundance Kid’ and John Wayne’s Oscar winning performance in ‘True Grit’, leading the pack.

In 1970 the Vietnam War was still raging on. The protests and demonstrations were still raging on.

In May 100,000 demonstrators descended on Washington D.C. to once again protest against the war.

On a brighter note, 600,000 music lovers attended 'The Isle of Wight Festival' in England. Some of the performers included Chicago, Richie Havens, John Sebastin, Joan Baez, Jethro Tull and Emerson, Lake and Palmer.

Unfortunately most of the music was heavily influenced by the war and drugs.

Chapter Twenty Four

'A Need To Be Creative'

The Holy Bible warns us about having too much pride. I could not help it, the Good Lord had blessed me with as perfect a life as anyone could hope for. I was healthy, I was happy, I was successful and I had a beautiful wife. I thanked and praised God every day for all that he had given me.

However as the weeks went by, I began to realize that there was something within me lacking. After much soul searching and personal inventory, I discovered what was missing. There was a creating deficient deep within me.

I had a need to create, to create for my own gratification. I decided that I needed to build yet another car. I needed to re-kindle all those feelings that I had experienced while building the '41 and the dragster.

I did not have that need for speed that I once had, I had been there, done that. For the first time I felt the need to create something 'outrageous'. Not

'Big Daddy Ed Roth' outrageous but still something that would turn heads. Something that would make people say 'hey! Look at that!'

I would have to give this a lot of thought, in the mean time life went on.

There was a bumper crop of great movies that year. 'Love Story' was the most talked about movie to come along in a long time. Before it was over Kathy was crying and I will admit I was teary-eyed.

Other big movies in 1970 include 'Airport',' Mash', 'Patton' and 'Five Easy Pieces'. It was also a great year for westerns, 'Little Big Man', 'The Ballad of Cable Hogue' and 'The Cheyenne Social Club'. John Wayne 'Duke' gave us two new westerns 'Chisum' and 'Rio Lobo'. Oh how could anyone forget Clint Eastwood's 'Two Mules for Sister Sara'.

A few days later, I took a stroll through the salvage yard. Nothing new about that except normally I was looking for something in particular, this time I was just letting my mind wander wherever it took me.

I mentally transformed and customized several of the older cars. For an example there was this 1950 Plymouth two door station wagon.

Mentally I cut the back three quarters of the roof off moving the top half of the rear windshield forward, hence making a pickup truck out of it. Then I yanked that very old and very tired old six cylinder engine out of it.
Then I install a 'hemi' engine and automatic transmission. I thought that maybe I paint it 'Plum Crazy' purple with a wild multi-colored flame job. Then I would install a set of 'stacks' to run the exhaust through. Next would come a set of mag wheels and wide tires.

Yeah it might be cool and it might even turn heads but it would not be outrageous.

A few days later I was back out in the 'bone' yard. Once again I was letting my imagination run wild.

This time I stopped in front of a 1957 Lincoln Premiere two door hardtop. This thing was incredibly long with huge tail fins and vertical Quad headlights. I envisioned sectioning this car by cutting 12" right out of the middle of it from bumper to bumper. Which would make the roof line one foot lower and make it look even longer than it was already.

Being a two door hardtop I couldn't figure out how to chop the top and with all that glass she would look strange but not outrageous.

The third time was a charm. I found myself looking at the most unlikely candidate of all. It was a 1959 Chevrolet four door Bel Aire. It wasn't nearly as long as the Lincoln but that was ok because now I wasn't thinking long I was thinking 'Short'.

In my mind's eye I had completely removed the top. Then I cut the car in half, removing about four feet right out of the center of the car. This moved the rear half forward considerably, then I took the four doors and made two out of them. I used the front half of the front doors and the rear half of the back doors.

We're talking two seat roadster here.

A couple of days later, I'm telling Hank all about it and then he says something that temporarily deflates my balloon. Won't work! Can't be done!

Those 59's have got a real weird assed 'X' frame and you can't shorten that!

Bill who had been just standing around listening, spoke up "You could put that body on a later model chassis. That would open up a whole world of possibilities. He was of course right I could choose to keep it all Chevrolet or literally put it on any chassis. Whatever it could/would give you a later model engine, transmission and rear end. It also would have bigger, better brakes and steering.

Out of curiosity Hank asks why a '59 Chevrolet anyway. They are God awful ugly. I replied that I have always loved those cat-eyed taillights, those long fins that go out instead of up and those horizontal headlights.

I told them that I was thinking about sinking the headlights and taillights about six inches. Roll the front and rear pans, pancake the hood and about a dozen more body modifications. I think that the overall package would look 'bitchin'.

Bill enquired as to just what some of those changes might be? Well sunken license plates front and rear. Sunken radio antennas through the rear fins and into the rear fenders, I would remove the door handles and most of the chrome trim.

I would enhance its already outrageous look, There I had said the 'O' word again.

Remembering 1971

1,200 inmates took thirty guards and other prison employees prisoners during a prison riot at the Attica State Prison in Buffalo, New York. It ended in a blood bath four days later with nine guards and twenty-eight inmates being killed in a hail of bullets from police gunfire.

The United States Supreme Court made a landmark ruling that desegregation was indeed constitutional.

In an attempt to shut down the Ho Chi minh trail (a North Vietnam supply route) South Vietnam and American forces invaded Laos. This turned out to be a dismal failure.

The most important medical breakthrough since the invention of the Xray was introduced. It was called Cat Scanning (computerizes Axial Tomography).

The Pittsburg Pirates became baseball's World Series Champions.

The Super Bowl was won by The Baltimore Colts.

Duane Allman of the famed 'Allman Brother Band' died in a motorcycle crash.

Have you ever wondered where the term 'Male Chauvinist Pig' came from? Kate Millet was the first person to string those words together when describing Norman Mailer.

The three most popular television shows were 'All in the Family', 'The Flip Wilson Show' and 'Marcus Welby M.D.'.

The biggest movies of the year included 'Two lane Blacktop', 'The Last Picture Show' and 'The French Connection'.

In Music the biggest hit singles were George Harrison's 'My Sweet Lord', John Lennon's 'Imagine', Rod Stewart's 'Maggie May', Lynn Anderson's 'Rose Garden', the Rolling Stone's 'Brown Sugar' and Don McLean's 'American Pie'.

Remembering 1972

The average cost of a new home was $27,550, split level homes were $32,400. You could buy a new Ford Pinto for $2,078 and gasoline was 55 cents a gallon.

Eight members of a group called 'Black September' (Arab gunmen) carrying AKM assault rifles killed eleven Israel athletes and one German policeman on September 6th. At the time of these attacks there were no fully trained professional counter-terrorism forces for the Olympics.

This was the same year as the 'Watergate' scandals. Five White House operatives burglarized and placed wiretaps in the offices of the Democratic National Committee. On September 15th the grand jury indicted the five along with E. Howard Hunt Jr. and G. Gordon Liddy for conspiracy, burglary and wiretapping.

On November 7th President Richard Nixon was re-elected in one of the largest landslides in American history.

President Nixon resigned on August 8th, twenty eight months after Watergate started.

On August 9th Gerald Ford becomes this counties next President.

On September 8th President Ford gives former President Nixon a full and complete pardon.

The Winter Olympics were held in Sapporo, Japan. These Olympics went off without a 'hitch'.

An earthquake in Bingol, Turkey killed over 1,000 people and left another 10,000 homeless. Another earthquake hit the town of Ghir, Iraq leaving another 5,000dead.

Three gun men open fire with automatic weapons at the Lod International Airport in Tel aviv, Israel killing twenty six and injuring dozens more.

Hurricane Agnes hit Pennsylvania, New York, Maryland and Virginia killing 117.

Another earthquake hits Nicaragua killing nearly 10,000.

Twenty two bombs exploded in Belfast, Ireland killing nine and seriously injuring 130.

The United States Senate passes the 'Equal Rights Amendment' making the sexes equal.

After anti war demonstrations which drew over 100,000 demonstrators, the last U.S. ground troops were withdrawn from Vietnam.
A dam breaks at Rapid City, South Dakota on June 9th killing over two hundred.

Arthur Bremer shoots Governor George Wallace three times on May 15th leaving him paralyzed.

A dam in Buffalo Creek Valley, West Virginia collapses and kills 118 people.

The best movies of the year include 'The God Father', 'Dirty Harry', 'Diamonds are Forever' and 'The Last Picture Show'.

The best television shows include 'Hawaii Five-O', 'The Brady Bunch' and 'Monty Python's Flying Circus'. This was also the first year for HBO (Home Box Office).

Some of the best songs were Chuck Berry's 'My Ding-A-Ling', Commander Cody's 'Hot Rod Lincoln', Neil Young's 'Heart of Gold', Robert John's 'the Lion Sleeps tonight', Ricky Nelson's 'Garden Party' and Elton John's 'Rocket Man'.

Remembering 1973

The average income in 1973 was $12,900. Like always some folks were living on next to nothing and some other folks were getting rich.

To give you an idea what cars were selling for, the AMC Javelin cost $2,900, while a Ford Galaxie 500 cost $3,883.

Gasoline was 40 cents a gallon and a dozen eggs brought 45 cents.

The average cost of a new home was $32,500.

The hot topics of conversation were Roe VS Wade. The Supreme Court made an abortion a US Constitutional Right. The Alaskan Oil Pipeline Bill passes congress and OPEC (Organization of Petroleum Exporting Countries) increased their prices 200%.

About 200 Oglala Sioux and the members of AIM (American Indian Movement) a militant civil rights organization started occupying 'Wounded Knee' an area on the Pine Ridge Indian Reservation for seventy one days.

The Indians and the federal authorities (U.S. Marshals and F.B.I.), exchanged regular gunfire with one another, with the Indians surrendering in May.

Wounded Knee has been a blight on American history since 1890. The U.S. Cavalry massacred 300 un-armed Sioux Indians there.

In Chicago, Illinois the 'Sears Tower' was completed making it the world's tallest building. It has 108 floors and is 1,729 feet tall. It was designed by architect Bruce Graham and engineer Fazlar Khan.

100,000 American workers lose their jobs when Chrysler and other US car makers close a number of plants.

The Sears Tower in Chicago loses its title 'World's Tallest Building' when the 'World Trade Center' opens in New York City.

The Spanish Prime Minister is assassinated by Basque Terrorists.

A Libyan passenger plane is shot down by Israel forces.

Secretariat wins the Triple Crown, the first horse to do so in twenty five years.
For seventy seven days the Mississippi River floods reaching its peak in St. Louis, Missouri.

Some of the best films include 'American Graffiti', 'The Sting', 'Deliverance' and 'The Lady Sings the Blues'.

The best television shows include Elvis Presley's 'Aloha from Hawaii' viewed by over one billion (that's with a 'B') people. 'The Partridge Family', 'McMillian and Wife', 'The Waltons' and M*A*S*H.

Some of the best songs were 'Tie a Yellow Ribbon Round the Ole Oak Tree' by Tony Orlando and Dawn. Jim Croce's 'Bad Bad Leroy Brown', Kristofferson's 'Why Me Lord', John Denver's 'Rocky Mountain High' and Charlie Rich's 'Behind Closed Doors'.

Remembering 1974

Inflation continues to spiral out of control not just here at home but around the world as well. A gallon of gasoline costs 55 cents and the average new car costs $3,750. The big bargain of the year was Chevrolet Vega selling at $2,617. The average yearly income was at $13,900. If you were renting a house the average was around $185 a month.

The IRA (Irish Republican Army) begins bombing everything in sight, from the 'Tower of London' to the 'House of Parliament' to dozens of pubs.

Here at home Richard Nixon becomes the first American president forced to resign the office.

President Ford enacts an amnesty program for Vietnam War deserters and draft evaders.

The Kooteni Native American Indian tribe declares war on the United States. The government bought the tribe off with 12 ½ acres of land, but a lot was learned about the woes of the tribe.

The Soviet Union successfully launches its first space station. Over the next two years Soviet crews docked there several times.

Farther in the year the global recession deepens causing among other things a gasoline shortage and much higher prices at the pump.

The world population reaches a swaggering four billion people.

In India nearly 20,000 people died from a small pox epidemic.

Here in the United States 148 tornadoes (the largest series of tornadoes in American history) hit thirteen states killing 315 people and injuring over 5,000 others.

India of all countries became the sixth country to detonate a nuclear weapon.

A wild fire (the worst in Argentine history) consumes 1.2 million acres.

A television show called ‘Happy Days’ (inspired by the movie ‘American Graffiti’) began an eleven year run on ABC.

Americans are fairly upset because the first class postage stamps raises in price 25%, they went from 8 cents to 10 cents.

A Turkish DC10 crashes in Paris, France and 346 people died in what became known as ‘the world’s worst air disaster.

200,000 fans attended a rock concert called ‘California Jam’ in Ontario.

On the 20th of April the ‘Northern Ireland Conflict’ claimed its 1,000th victim.

Another airplane crashes into the mountains of Bali, a Pan Am 707 killing 107 people.

40,000 people were killed on August 15th by a hurricane and floods in Bangladesh. Another 5,000 people die when hurricane Fifi strikes Honduras with 110 MPH winds.

Nolan Ryan playing for the 'California Angels' throws the fastest recorded pitch at 100.9 MPH.

Yet another airliner crashes and kills 191 people in Sri Lanka, it was a Dutch DC8.

Some of the best movies of the year include 'Blazing Saddles', 'the Life and Times of Grizzly Adams', 'Chinatown', 'the Longest Yard' and 'the Towering Inferno'.

Best television programming includes 'Gunsmoke', 'Kung Fu', 'the Rookies', 'Adam 12', 'Barnaby Jones' and 'the Six Million Dollar Man'.

Top hits included Cat Stevens 'Cats in the Cradle', Ray Steven's 'the Streak', Charlie Rich's 'the Most Beautiful Girl', Jim Croce's 'Time in a Bottle' and the Righteous Brother's 'Rock and Roll Heaven'.

Remembering 1975

This was not a good year for England. Their yearly inflation rate was 24.2%, while here in the United States our inflation rate was 9.2% and most of us thought that was too high. Just to illustrate a point, Gasoline here at home was selling for44 cents a gallon while it brought 72 cents in England.

The average cost of a new car (US) was $4,250. Pontiac Ventura Couples sold for $3,829. While Oldsmobile Delta 88 Royale's brought $5, 626.

The average American income was $14,100 which was $200 more than 1974.

This was the year that Bill Gates and Paul Allen started Microsoft.

Middle Eastern oil producing countries (OPEC) raises crude oil prices by 10%. World Wide crude oil goes to over $13 a barrel.

With no one left to help South Vietnam protect itself against the Northern aggressor, a war which had lasted for twenty years sadly ends in bitter defeat.

At this point the only involvement the US had in Vietnam was a program called 'Operation Babylift'. We bought countless thousands of Vietnamese orphans to the US.

President Gerald Ford signs a $2.3 billion dollar loan to keep New York City out of the bankruptcy court.

If England didn't already have enough problems the IRA seemed to rear its ugly head everywhere. They killed Ross Mcwhirter the co-founder of the Guinness Book of Records. They bombed the London Hilton Hotel in Park Lane. An IRA hit squad took refuse and hostages at Balcombe Street in Central London.

350,000 unarmed Moroccans cross the border into the Spanish controlled Sahara Desert. This action became known as the 'Green March'.

Here in the US believe it or not doctors went on strike. About all this caused was for hospitals to reduce patient services.

Meanwhile back in England, Dutch Elm disease destroys more than three million Elm trees. As Great Britain's inflation rate jumps 25%, The UK implements the sex discrimination and equal pay act.

Jimmy Hoffa ex-teamster boss just vanishes into thin air never to be seen or heard of again.

If that's not bizarre enough for you, newspaper heiress Patty Hearst (who already had all the money in the world) joins the SLA (Symbionese Liberation Army) and freely participates in an armed robbery of a bank in San Francisco.

Miss Hearst quickly becomes America's Most Wanted criminal. She was arrested, tried, convicted and she served two years before having her sins pardoned by President Bill Clinton.

Some of this year's best movies included blockbuster 'Jaws', 'One flew over the Cuckoo's nest', 'Dog Day Afternoon', 'Monty Python and the

Holy Grail', 'Shampoo' and 'the Apple Dumpling Gang'.

Favorite television shows included the newly created 'Saturday Night Live', 'All in the Family', 'Sanford and Son', 'Laverne and Shirley', 'Starsky and Hutch', 'Rich Man, Poor Man', 'the Six Million Dollar man' and 'Bionic Woman'.

The hit songs that we all enjoyed, Ethan John's 'Lucy in the Sky with Diamonds', the Eagle's 'Best of My Love', John Denver's 'Thank God I'm a Country Boy', Glen Campbell's 'Rhinestone Cowboy' and the Captain and Tennille's 'Love Will Keep Us Together'.

Remembering 1976

The United States celebrates its 200th birthday of its independence from British rule.

The yearly inflation rate dropped from 9.2% in '75 to 5.75% in 1975.

The average cost of a gallon of gasoline was 59 cents, which was up 15 cents per gallon in 1976.

There was an earthquake in Tabgshan, China which took 655,000 human lives.

A tidal wave hit the Philippines killing another 5,000 people.

In 1975 Microsoft was started, 1976 was the year Steve Jobs and Steve Wozniak started 'Apple'. Apple Initially Struggled to survive, today Apple is worth over 700 billion dollars.

The CN Tower in Toronto, Canada was for several years 'the tallest free standing structure in the world, It stands 1,815 feet tall.

Concorde air flights from London to New York City had a flying time of just under3 hours. That was half the time of other aircraft. The Concorde had a cruising speed of 1,350 MPH.

1976 gave us a new President. President Jimmy Carter who's claim to fame was that of a one term Governor and peanut farmer from Plains, Georgia. Carter won the presidency over Gerald Ford.

Here's an interesting note, Gerald Ford served as both Vice President and President of these United States and was never elected to either position.

Hurricane Belle hit the north half of the East Coast. It was destructive to property but little else.

An earthquake hit Guatemala and Honduras killing more than 22.000 people.

First case of legionnaire's disease affected 4,000 delegates in Pennsylvania on July 23rd.

Two passenger jets collided over Zagreb, Yugoslavia due to the errors of air traffic controllers.

Howard Hughes American Billionaire dies at the age of 70. He had been a recluse for over 20 years.

An un-marked space probe, Viking 1 lands on Mars and for six years send back data.

The best selling car of the year was the Oldsmobile Cutlass. The Cutlass sold for $4, 775. In comparison a Plymouth Arrow could have been bought for $3,175.

Some of the best movies of the year included 'Rocky', 'the Outlaw Josie Wales', 'Taxi Driver' and 'All the President's Men'.

Some of the best television watching was ABC's 'Welcome back Kotter' and 'Barney Miller'. On CBS there was 'Kojac' and 'Barnaby Jones'. NBC was showing 'Chico and the Man', 'The Rockford Files', 'Police Woman' and 'The Little House on the Prairie'.

Some of the hit songs that we listened to were Paul Simon's '50 Ways to Leave Your Lover', the Eagle's 'Take it to the Limit', Fleetwood Mac's 'Say You Love Me' and the Beach Boys 'Rock and Roll Music'.

Remembering 1977

I've always heard it said that a person's rent or mortgage payment plus utilities should not exceed one fourth of their income. If that indeed is a good formula Then 1977 was a fair year. The average income was down $100, It went from $16,000 in 1976 to $15,000 in 1977.

The average monthly rent was $240 per month.

The price of gasoline was 65 cents, 6 cents higher that 1976's 59 cents.

On July 13th Several horrendous lightning strives caused a twenty-five hour 'black out' in New York City. When electrical power is denied to millions of people here is what happens. (1) LaGuardia and Kennedy Airports are shut down for over eight hours. (2) Most New York television stations were off the air. (3) 4,000 people were trapped in the subway stations and had to be evacuated. (4) In every poor neighborhood in the city there was wide spread looting, vandalism and arson. (5) 1,616 stores were damaged, because of the rioting. (6) Police Arrested 4,500 looters and in the process 550 police officers were injured. It was said it the time that without air conditioning and with a heat wave going on, the natives just went a little crazy.

At the young age of forty two (42) the 'King of Rock and Roll' Elvis Presley died in what was thought to be a heart attack. After struggling with drug abuse, health problems and a divorce from the love of his life Priscilla, Elvis leaves this world.

After massive protests and riots by the Panamanian people, the United States relinquishes control of the Panama Canal, which it had built fifty years earlier.

On May 28th, 165 people died in a fire of a Beverly Hills Supper Club.

Three days later, The Trans Alaskan Pipeline opens carrying seven hundred thousand (700,000) barrels of crude oil per day. The construction of the pipeline started in 1973 in answer to OPEC's announcement of a 70% price increase.

President Carter warns the American people to make changes in their oil consumption.

President Carter grants pardons to all those Americans who dodged the draft during the Vietnam era.

1,500 People lose their lives in a earthquake in Bucharest, Romania.

A cyclone hits India killing 20,000 people and left two million others homeless.

Race horse Seattle Slew became the 10th horse to win The Triple Crown.

Two jumbo jets collide at Tenerife Airport in the Canary Islands.

The big movies of the year were 'Star Wars IV', 'Smokey and the Bandit', 'King Kong' and 'Saturday Night Fever'.

Some of the television shows worth mentioning are ABC's 'High School Rock', 'Baretta' and 'Charlie's Angels'. CBS's 'Wonder Woman', 'Maude', 'Rhoda' and 'The Jefferson's'. NBC's 'McCloud', 'Wheel of Fortune' and the 'Gong Show'.

Hit songs included Rod Stewart's 'Tonight's the night', Stevie Wonder's 'The Wish', Glen Campbell's 'Southern Lights', The Eagle's 'Hotel California' and Fleetwood Mac's 'Dreams'.

Remembering 1978

The average yearly income was up $2,000 to $17,000. Everything increases in price just as it was expected.

The average price of a new house was $54,800 while the average cost of a used home was $13,650. The price of renting increases slightly to $260 per month.

The price of a gallon of gasoline was 63 cents.

The thirty one year old war between Israel and Egypt came to an end. This new peace came largely because of one man, President Carter.

A helium filled balloon 'Double Eagle II' carried three men across the Atlantic Ocean. They traveled 3,000 miles in 137 hours from Maine to France.

US teachers strike giving thousands of students an extended summer vacation.

The Volkswagen Beetle after manufacturing 20 million cars over the past thirty (30) years abruptly stops.

World- wide employment rises sharply after decades of near full employment.

The price of gold reaches $200 an ounce for the first time.

With gasoline selling at a premium, cheap Japanese cars are flooding the US car market.

An oil slick 18 miles wide and 80 miles long is created when the Amoco Cadiz runs aground on the coast of Brittany.

Two million people are left homeless in India after the worst monsoon of the season hits.

20,000 people are killed after an earthquake strikes Tabas, Iran.

After a sordid love affair with a fourteen year old girl, Roman Polanski flees to France before US authorities could prosecute.

900 followers of cult leader Jim Jones commit suicide in Guyana, Lebanon.

The Big movies of the year included 'Grease', 'Close encounters of the Third Kind', 'The Deer Hunter' and 'National Lampoon's Animal House'.
On television we watched 'The Love Boat', 'Three's Company', 'Chips' and Quincy M.D.

The music that we listened to included The Bee Gee's 'Night Fever', The Commodores 'Three Times a Lady', Johnny Mathis and Denise Williams 'Too much, Too Little, Too Late' and Kenny Loggins and Stevie Nick's 'Whenever I call you Friend'.

Remembering 1979

The American Inflation rate was 11.2% while Great Britain was suffering with an inflation rate of 17%. Here in the US wages and the cost of goods both were steadily rising.

Mercury Cougar XR7's were selling for $6,430, while the cost of a gallon of gasoline to push it was selling at an average cost of 86 cents. That same gallon of gasoline went much farther in a Toyota Corolla which sold for $3,698.

Margaret Thatcher was the first woman to ever be elected Prime Minister of Great Britain.

The IRA bombings in England continued with the assassination of Lord Louis Mountbatten. He was both the Queens cousin and an Admiral of the British fleet.

The USSR invades Afghanistan, ten years later and with a death toll of 15,000 Soviet troops they retreated from what they called an unwinnable war.

After fifteen years of exile Ayatollah Ruhollah Khomeni returns to Tehran, Iran and seizes all power. His first order was to deport all foreigners forcing over 1,000 US State Department employees to leave the country. Ninety other Americans were taken hostage at the American Embassy.

The US and the Soviet Union signed the SALT II treaty, limiting arms production on both sides.

A nuclear reactor fire in Pennsylvania caused the now famous 'Three Mile Island Nuclear Accident'.

1979 became known as the 'Year of the Tornadoes' here in the US. 855 tornadoes killed 58 people and injured over 2,000.

In Saudi Arabia 400 armed Islamic Muslins seized the Grand Mosque in Mecca. Two weeks later more than 250 were dead.

A mob attack destroys the US Embassy in Islamabad, Pakistan.

Saddam Hussein becomes the President of Iraq.

In Northern Ireland eighteen British Soldiers are murdered at Warrenpoint, South Down.

A tsunami hits Nice, France killing twenty three people.

American Airlines flight 191 crashes and burns near O'Hare Airport in Chicago.

This year's top movies included 'Kramer Vs Kramer', 'Superman the Movie', 'Rocky II' and 'Moonraker'.

Some of the most watched television 'Mork and Mindy', 'Taxi', 'Dallas', 'Three's Company' and 'The Walton's'.

Hit songs included Donna Summer's 'Bad Girls', the Village People's 'Y.M.C.A.', Elton John's 'Mama Can't Buy You Love' and Kenny Roger's 'the Gambler'.

Remembering 1980

This was the beginnings of 'the electronic world' in which you and I live in today. Bigger and bigger televisions, etc! Smaller and smaller mobile devises.

1980's inflation rate was 13.58%. A used home had an average price of $13,650 or would rent for an average of $300 per month. While the average new home sold for $68,700.

The average income was $19,500 per year. The average cost of a new car was $7,200, to put this into perspective a Pontiac Firebird sold for $5,992 and a gallon of gasoline cost $1.19.

The Iraqi dictator Saddam Hussein attacks his neighbor Iran. A bloody war that lasted for ten years and an estimated one million people lost their lives.

Ted Turner launches a new 24 hour news network called CNN (cable news network). CNN was slow to take off but later became a news giant.

Ronald Reagan became America's latest President.

Japan becomes the world's largest manufacture of automobiles.

There was a mass exodus from Cuba into the United States they came by the thousands on anything that would float. They were considered 'Political Refuses'.

Mount St. Helens erupts in Washington state killing 57.

A severe heat wave in the southern US, kills 1,117.

The US oil companies were making so much money that the government passed the 'Crude Oil Windfall Profit Tax Act'.

The world is shocked by the senseless shooting death of former Beetles John Lennon.

A fire destroys the MGM Grand Hotel in Las Vegas.

A 6.0 earthquake in southern Italy kills more than 3,000 people.

Most watched movies included ‘Star Wars V’, ‘Superman II’, ‘Nine to Five’, ‘Raging Bull’ and ‘Coal Miner’s Daughter’.

On television we watched ‘The A-Team’, BJ and the Bear’, Cagney and Lacey’ and ‘Dallas’ answers who shot JR.

Popular Songs that we listened to included Blondie’s ‘Call me’, Billy Joel’s ‘It’s Still Rock and Roll to me’, Olivia Newton John’s ‘Magic’ and Christopher Cross’s ‘Ride Like the Wind’.

Remembering 1981

The average yearly income was up to $21, 050. The yearly inflation rate was down over 3% to 10.35%. The prices of goods had fairly well leveled off.

Iran Released 52 American hostages that they had held for 444 days.

In England the government under Prime Minister Thatcher creates an economic revival called the 'Privatization of Nationalized Industries'.

Here in the US, the air traffic controllers went on strike, so President Reagan just fired them all.

In Northern Ireland Bobby Sands (an Irish Republican Army Member) was elected to Westminster as the MP for Fermanagh and South Tyrone. About that same time he died from a hunger strike.

The military leaders of Poland declared Martial Law. The government said that it was necessary to prevent a civil war.

Anti nuclear protestors invaded the Diablo Canyon Nuclear Reactor in California.

US researchers find the remains of the 'Titanic' in the North Atlantic.

The US Supreme ruled that parents must be notified when their daughter are seeking an abortion.

Grease has an earthquake at Athens which killed sixteen people.

In Rome an assassination attempt on Pope John Paul II was unsuccessful. He was shot but didn't die.

In Egypt President Anwar Sadat was assassinated.

In the US Sandra Day O'Connor was nominated to become the first female justice to the Supreme Court.

President Ziaur Rahman was assassinated in Bangladesh.

The big movies of the year included ‘Raiders of the lost Ark’, ‘On Golden Pond’, ‘Chariots of Fire’, ‘Authur’ and ‘Cannon ball Run’.

Television shows included ‘Archie Bunkers Place’, Fantasy Island’, ‘Magnum P.I.’ and ‘Trapper John M.D.’.

Popular songs, John Lennon’s ‘(just like) Starting Over’, Dolly Parton’s ‘Nine to Five’, Eddie Rabbit’s ‘I Love a Rainy Night’ and REO Speed wagon’s ‘Keep on Loving You’

Remembering 1982

The yearly inflation rate drops another 4% to 6.16%. The average yearly wage stayed at $21,050. A new GMC pickup Truck sold for $5,400 and a gallon of gasoline was 91 cents.

The average house sold for $23,644 and would have rented for $320 per month.

Carlos the Jackal commits a wave of terrorist attacks on France.

The Falkland Islands/Maldives are invaded by Argentina. England sends her Navy and Air Force and retakes possession.

$9,800,000 (nine million eight hundred thousand) is stolen from an armored car in New York.

US Government breaks up the AT&T monopoly, it split into seven different companies.

Another year of IRA bombings in London and all over England.

700,000 (seven hundred thousand) demonstrators protested at New York City's Central Park.

Commercial Whaling is stopped by the International Whaling Commission.

The first permanent artificial heart (developed by Robert Jarvis) is successfully implanted.

A severe recession begins here at home in the US.

The 'Ocean Ranger' (the world's largest oil rig) sinks in the North Atlantic.

The Vietnam Veterans Memorial is dedicated in Washington D.C.

Thousands of people are killed in Southern Mexico after earthquakes and volcanic eruptions.

Twenty million Elm trees die from Dutch elm disease in England.

The big movies included ‘E.T. the Extra- Terrestrial’, Rocky III’, ‘Porky’s’, ‘an Officer and a Gentleman’, ‘the Best Little Whorehouse in Texas’, and ‘Star Trek II the Wrath of Knan.

Some of the best television shows included ‘Dynasty’, ‘Falcon Crest’, ‘Hill Street Blues’ and ‘Knight Rider’.

Some of the year’s best songs Survivor’s ‘Eye of the Tiger’, John Cougar’s ‘Hurts so Good’, Willie Nelson’s ‘Always on my Mind’. Huey Lewis and the News’s ‘Do you Believe in love’ and Kenny Roger’s ‘Love will turn You Around’.

Remembering 1983

The US employment rises to over 12 (twelve) million people, the highest rate since 1941. The yearly inflation rate drops to 3.22% as the price of goods continually rise. Those lucky enough to be working are earning an average wage of $21,070.

A new Mustang sold for $6,572 compared to a Volkswagen Rabbit at $6, 994. A Dodge Ram 50 pickup truck sold for $5,665.

The US Embassy at Beirut, Lebanon is bombed killing 63 people.

In England the IRA continues bombing, a bomb explodes outside of Harrods on December 17th.

Hurricane Alicia hits the Texas coast and twenty-one people are killed.

Over 4,000,000 (four Million) people die in Ethiopia as they reached out for world aid.

In the Philippines, the opposition leader Benigno Aquino is assassinated.

The government of Granada is overthrown by Cuban Troops. President Reagan sent 5,000 Marines to take it back, nineteen US troops were killed.

In England, $37.5 million ($37,500,000) dollars worth of gold bars were stolen at Heathrow Airport. In case you were wondering, the gold bars weighed over three tons (6,000 pounds).

In the general elections in England, Margaret Thatcher wins by a landslide.

Barney Clark the first person to receive an artificial heart died after 112 days.

The big movies included 'Tootsie', 'Trading Places', 'WarGames', 'Flashdance', 'Terms of Endearment', National Lampoon's Vacation' and 'Educating Rita'.

Television included 'Mash' (the final episode was watched by 125 million people), 'Cheers', 'Dynasty', 'High Performance', 'Remington Steele' and 'St. Elsewhere'.

Best Songs included The Police's 'Every Breath You Take', Hall and Oakes's 'Maneater', Bob Seger and the Silver Bullet Band's 'Shame on the Moon', Marvin Gaye's 'Sexual Healing' and Kenny Loggin's 'Heart to Heart'.

Remembering 1984

Recession continues to be problematic in the US as over seventy banks fail. The yearly inflation rate rises slightly higher to 4.3%.

The days of the five or six thousand dollar car or truck were long gone. The Dodge Ram 50 was selling for $8,995 which was more than $3,000 over 1983's price. Chrysler New Yorkers were bringing $13,045, while a new Corvette sold for $23,392.

The average yearly income was slightly higher at $21,600. While the average house sold for $37,182, which would rent for $350 per month.

Indian Prime Minister Indira Gandhi was assassinated. She was India's first female Prime Minister and she had been elected to four terms.

Also in India, 3,500 people were killed due to a toxic gas leak at the Bhopac Union Carbide Factory.

In Mexico City, 500 people died in a giant gas explosion at the Pemex storage facility.

A terrorist shoots and kills twenty and wounds sixteen more at McDonalds in San Ysidroc, Ca.

In England the 700 year old wing of York Minster was destroyed by fire.

Typhoon Ike strikes the Philippines killing over 3,000 people.

Paul McCarthy, David Bowie, George Michaels, James Taylor, Phil Collins and over forty other singers came together for a one time recording session. They raised millions of dollars for the Famine Relief in Ethiopia.

Best movies of the year included 'Ghostbusters', Indiana Jones and the Temple of Doom', 'Gremlins', 'Beverly Hills Cop', 'The Karate Kid', 'The Terminator' and 'The Killing Fields'.

On television we watched 'Entertainment Tonight', 'Hill Street Blues', 'Fame', 'Magnum P.I.' and 'The A-Team'.

We listened to Michael Jackson's 'Thriller' which sold over 37 million copies, Bruce Springsteen's 'Dancing in the Dark', Elton John's 'I Guess that's why they call it the Blues', Huey Lewis and the news's 'the Heart of Rock & Roll' and ZZ Top's 'Legs'.

Remembering 1985

The yearly inflation rate, average yearly wages and the price of homes, cars and goods in general remain pretty much the same as last year.

The Eastern half of the US suffers from one of the coldest winters ever recorded.

Armero, Colombia had a volcanic eruption that killed 23,000 people.

Palestinian terrorists hijacked the Italian cruise liner 'Achille Lauro'.

In Malta, an Egypt Air flight 648 is hijacked and 56 people are killed.

TWA flight 847 is hijacked by Shiite Hezbollah terrorists.

In Rome and Vienna terrorist gunmen shot passengers at the airports.

French agents planted two bombs on the Greenpeace ship "Rainbow Warrior' and sunk the ship at New Zealand.

The 2,448 mile 'Route 66' which was established in 1926 is removed from the highway system.

Mexico City had an 8.1 earthquake which killed over 9,000 people.

A mostly black group MOVE in Philadelphia was bombed by the police department. The C4 and Tovex bomb burned down 53 houses leaving 240 people homeless. The blast killed six adults and four children.

A Boeing 747 flight 123 crashes into Mount Osutaka, Japan.

A massive car bomb kills 45 and injured 175 people in Beirut, Lebanon.

Ray Charles, Willie Nelson, Bob Dylan, Billy Joel, Lionel Richie, Kenny Rogers and dozens of other performers record 'We Are the World' to raise money for famine relief.

Big movies ‘Back to the Future’, Cocoon’, ‘the Color Purple’, ‘Out of Africa’, ‘Rambo First Blood II’ and ‘a View to a kill’.

Television ‘Moonlighting’, ‘Larry King Live’, ‘Stingray’, ‘West 57th’, ‘Hell town’, ‘the Golden Girls’ and ‘MacGyver’.

Songs included Foreigner’s ‘I Want to Know What Love is’, ‘Huey Lewis and the News’s ‘the Power of Love’, Stevie Wonder’s ‘Part-time Lover’, Whitney Houston’s ‘You Give Good Love’, and John Cougar Mellencamp’s ‘Lonely Ol’ Night’.

Remembering 1986

Believe it or not, 1.91% yearly inflation with an average wage of $22,400. The average cost of a home was $44,040, which would rent for $385 per month.

The price of a gallon of gasoline was down to 89 cents. A new Plymouth Colt sold for $4,999, while a new Ford Mustang brought $7,452.

US bombs Libya in protest their involvement in the bombing of a crowded La Belle Disco in Berlin, Germany.

The Soviet Nuclear Reactor at Chernobyl explodes spreading radioactive material across most of Europe. Hundreds of thousands of people were displaced.

6.5 million Americans paid $10 each to participate in a huge charity event called 'Hands across America'. Americans held hands forming a human chain across this country. The money went to fight poverty through local charities.

The US Space Shuttle Challenger disintegrates 73 seconds after launching killing all seven astronauts.

Pan Am flight 73 with 358 passengers was hijacked at Karachi International Airport in Pakistan.

A bomb explodes on a TWA jet over Greece and four passengers are sucked out of a hole.

1500 people are killed by a 7.5 earthquake in El Salvador.

157 people died in Britain from 'Mad Cow Disease'.

175 gold miners die in Kinross Mine in Eastern Transvaal, South Africa.

Lethal gas from the volcanic lake Nyos in Cameroon, West Africa kills 1,500 people.

Big movies 'Top gun', 'Crocodile Dundee', 'Platoon', 'Aliens', 'Star Trek IV' and 'the Color of Money'.

Television 'Highway to Heaven', 'the Twilight Zone', 'Murder She Wrote', 'Fame', 'Growing Pains', and 'Family Ties'.

Music Cyndi Lauper's 'True Colors', 'Kenny Loggin's 'Danger Zone', Stevie Nicks's 'Talk to me", 'Tina Turner's 'Typical Male' and The Cars 'Tonight She Comes'.

Remembering 1987

Yearly inflation was up to 3.66% and the average income was also up to $24,350. Housing costs and rent are about the same as last year.

Chevrolet cavalier sold for $7,395 while the top of the line Caprice brought $12,510. Ford Escort sold for $6,895 and the Taurus brought $11,808.

The US stock market crashes on October 19th, 508 point drop or 22.6%. Stock markets around the world followed suit.

In England, 31 people died in a fire at Kings Cross tube station.

On June 12th President Reagan delivered his now famous ‘tear down that wall’ speech.

37 US sailors are killed on the USS Shark by an air to sea missile. Iraq claimed that it was an accident.

Terry Waite envoy of the Archbishop of Canterbury is kidnapped in Beirut, Lebanon. He was held for 1, 763 days (over 4 years) before being released.

The World's population reaches five billion (5,000,000,000).

A cross-channel ferry capsizes and kills 193 passengers and crew at Zeebrugge, Belgium.

The fastest train in the world was Britain's inner-city train travelling at 148 miles per hour.

The United Kingdom re-elects Margaret Thatcher for the third time.

More than a hundred people were killed at Tamil Tigers Plant in Colombo by a massive bomb.

In the United Kingdom Michael Ryan kills sixteen people with an assault rifle.

23 people are killed by hurricane winds south of England, it was the worst storm in 200 years.

A super typhoon kills 1,000 people in the Philippines submerging 14 fishing villages. Also in the Philippines a ferry accident kills four thousand (4,000) people.

Movies 'Three Men and a Baby', 'Fatal Attraction', 'Good Morning Vietnam', 'the Untouchables', 'Lethal Weapon' and 'Dirty Dancing'.

Television 'Jake and the Fat Man', '21 Jump Street', 'Married with Children', 'Rescue 911', 'Full house' and 'Thirty Something'.

Music Bob Segar's 'Shakedown', 'Billy Idol's 'Mony, Momy', Madonna's 'Causing a Commotion', Fleetwood Mac's 'Little Lies', Bon Jovi's 'Wanted Dead or Alive' and Kool and the Gang's 'Victory'.

Remembering 1988

The yearly inflation rate was up to 4.08% with an average yearly income of $24,450. An average monthly rent was around $420 and the average cost of a new car was $10,400. A new Ford Taurus sold for $9,996 and a Volkswagen Rabbit brought $7,104. A gallon of gasoline sold for 91 cents while a gallon of milk was $1.89.

In Burma over one million people demonstrated against military rule. The protests lasted for over a month and martial law was enacted.

Iraq carries out poison gas attacks on the Kurds. After eight years of fighting and with one and a half million dead the Iran-Iraq war finally ends.

In Armenia 60,000 people died from an earthquake.

A terrorist bomb explodes on a Pan Am jet over Lockerbie, Scotland killing 259 on board and another 11 on the ground.

In the UK, 34 people died in the Chapham Rail Crash.

Panama leader General Noriega was charged with drug smuggling and money laundering.

The USS Vincennes shot down an Iranian passenger jet flight 655 killing 290 passengers and crew.

Fires and droughts destroyed (793,880 acres) one third of Yellowstone National Park.

Hurricane Gilbert devastated Jamaica causing 7.1 billion in damages and killed 318 people.

Movies included 'Rain Man', 'Die Hard', 'Who Framed Roger Rabbit?', 'Big' and 'a Fish named Wanda'.

Television '48 Hours', 'the Wonder Years', 'America's Most Wanted', 'in the Heat of the Night', 'China Beach' and 'Murphy's Law'.

Music George Michael's 'Faith', Guns n' Rose's 'Sweet Child of Mine', Cheap Trick's 'the Flame', Billy Ocean's 'Get outta my dreams, Get into My

Car', Phil Collin's 'a Groovy Kind of Love' and Chicago's 'I Don't wanna live Without Your Love'.

Remembering 1989

The average cost of a new car jumps over 50% to $15,350 over $10,400 in 1988. New Ford Probe's sold for $12,695 while a new BMW 325's were $21,400. The average yearly inflation is only up .75% at 4.83%. The average yearly wage is up a little over 10% at $27, 450 which is $3,000 more than 1988.

In Iran the Ayatollah Khomeini is dead at the age of 86. He was the supreme leader since 1979 with the overthrow of Shaw Mohammad Reza Pahlavi, establishing the first Islamic Republic.

In Worsen, South Africa over 2,500 people are killed in violence.

In Czechoslovakia free elections are held after 200,000 people protested in Prague calling for an end to the countries Communist Government.

After 30 years of a Cold War between the US and the USSR it comes to an end. Massive protests on both sides of the 'Berlin Wall' bring about its eventual dismantling and the opening of the Brandenburg Gate. The East Berlin Government collapses and the City of Berlin becomes one.

In Beijing, China thousands of students protest for democracy in Tiananmen Square. The Chinese government declares martial law and hundreds of protestors are killed. As a result the US and many other countries placed sanctions on China.

George Bush Sr. becomes the new President of the United States.

A violent tornado killed 1,300 in Saturia, Bangladesh.

In Alaska the Exxon Valdez ran aground spilling 240,000 barrels of oil, that's 11 million gallons.

200 people were injured and 96 people were crushed to death in Sheffield, England at the Hillsborough Stadium during a sporting event.

51 People dead when a Marchioness Pleasure boat collided with a barge on the river Thames.

A 7.1 earthquake strikes the San Francisco Bay area killing 63 people.

Hurricane Hugo strikes from Puerto Rico to North Carolina killing over 80 people.

The US government spends 150 billion to bail out the Savings and Loan companies.

Big movies 'Batman', 'Indiana Jones and the Last Crusade', 'Lethal Weapon II', 'Driving Miss Daisy', 'License to Kill' and 'When Harry Met Sally'.

Television 'Cops', 'Quantum Leap', 'Seinfield', 'the Young Riders', 'Baywatch' and 'Mancuso, FBI'.

Music Chicago's 'Look Away', Paula Abdul's 'Straight Up', Debbie Gibson's 'Lost in Your Eyes', Bon Jovi's 'I'll be There for You' and New Kids on the Block's 'You Got It (the right stuff)'.

Remembering 1990

The US average yearly inflation rate goes up to 5.39% just slightly more than 1989. The average yearly income is up to $28,960 another $1,500 over the year before. Average monthly rent was $465 and a gallon of gasoline cost $1.34. A new Isuzu Rodeo sold for $12,490.

North and South Yemen unite and become one country, the Republic of Yemen.

No longer at war with Iran, Saddam Hussein of Iraq invades Kuwait. The US and the UK sent troops to Kuwait, for the US this begins Operation 'Desert Shield'.

In South Dakota the most complete skeleton of a T-Rex is found.

A major earthquake hit Iran killing over 50,000 people.

The US enters into a major recession that effects the economy of every country in the world.

John M. Poindexter (former US National Security Advisor) is convicted on multiple felony count

After several terms as UK Prime Minister Margaret Thatcher Resigns.

1,400 people died in Saudi Arabia in a stampede of people in a pedestrian tunnel.

89 people died in a fire at 'Happy Land' a social club in New York City.

In Italy they closed the 'Leaning Tower of Pisa' in fear of it falling over.

1,600 people were killed by a 7.7 earthquake in the Phipippines.

With Germany united it has a new government with new currency and new economics.

The UK imposes a new poll tax which is met head-on by massive demonstrations.

After 18 years in space the US Probe Pioneer reaches a distance of 46.5 billion miles.

Movies ‘Twin Peaks’, ‘Home Alone’, ‘Ghost’, ‘Dances With Wolves’, ‘Pretty Woman’, ‘Total Recall’ and ‘the Hunt for Red October’.

Television ‘Rodeo Drive’, ‘Carol and Company’, ‘Twin Peaks’, ‘Northern Exposure’, ‘the Fresh Prince of Bel-Air’ and ‘Beverly Hills 90210’.

Music Michael Bolton’s ‘How am I Suppose to Live without you’, Mariah Carey’s ‘Visions of Love’, Jon Bon Jovi’s ‘Blaze of Glory’, George Michael’s ‘Praying for Time’, Amy Grant’s ‘Baby Baby’ and Paula Abdul’s ‘the Promise of a New Day’.

Remembering 1991

The average yearly inflation rate was 4.25% with an average yearly wage of $29,430. The average monthly rent was $495 and a gallon of gasoline sold for $1.12.

Operation Desert Storm was a United Nations Coalition Force which included the US and many Arab and European countries. They bombed Iraq forces for over a month before Iraq pulled out.

200,000 people were killed by a cyclone in Bangladesh.

Thousands of homes were destroyed by fire in the hills of Oakland, California, where 25 people lost their lives.

Uzbekistan, Tajikstan, Kyrgyzstan, Axerbaijan, Ukraine, Moldova, Lithuania, Latvia, Belarus and Estonia all gained their independence with the dissolving of the USSR.

With 50% or more of India's population living below the poverty level, Ravia Gandhi the Prime Minister was assassinated.

In South Africa Winnie Mandela (wife of Nelson Mandela) was given a six year prison sentence for kidnapping four youths.

Seventy tornadoes break out in the central United States killing 17 people.

2,000 people died when a 7.0 earthquake hits Northern Italy.

In Indonesia 250 Timorese protestors were killed by the government at the Santa Cruz Cemetery.

Police brutality caught on film in California when they arrested Rodney King.

Three more countries won their independence from Yugoslavia. They were Macedonia, Croatia and Slovenia.

Movies 'Robin Hood: Prince of Thieves', 'the Silence of the Lambs', 'Hook', 'Father of the Bride', and 'Thelma and Louise'.

Television “Blossom’, ‘Harry and the Henderson’s’, ‘American Detective’, ‘C. Everett Koop M.D.’, ‘Home Improvement’ and ‘Reasonable Doubts’.

Music Mariah Carey’s ‘Someday’, Whitney Houston’s ‘all the Man that I Need’, Luther Vandross’s ‘Power of Love’, Michael Bolton’s ‘Love is a Wonderful Thing’ and Rod Stewart’s ‘Rhythm of My Heart’.

Remembering 1992

The yearly inflation rate was down 1.22% which made it 3.03%. The average yearly income was at $30,030, with houses renting for on the average at $519 per month. The average cost of a new car was $16,950. A new Buick Century was $18,199 and the Park Ave model sold for close to $30,000. A gallon of gasoline costs $1.05.

The US and the UN intervenes to help end the famine and civil war in Somalia with 'Operation Restore Hope'.

Bosnia and Herzegovina declare their dependence sparking a three year war between Muslins, Serbs and Croats.

Over 500 people were killed by a 6.8 earthquake in Turkey.

A sewer explodes in Guadalajara, Mexico killing 215 people and injuring 1,500 more.

Here in the US, Mafia crime boss John Gotti is sentenced to life in prison for conspiracy to commit murder and racketeering.

A 1.95 billion dollar flood in Chicago was created by a ruptured tunnel allowing the river to push through.

2,000 lives were lost during rioting in India after Hindu militants torn down the Babri Mosque.

The largest American shopping mall was built in Minnesota, it carried 78 acres.

Wide spread rioting breaks out in Los Angeles after the acquittal of the four police officers who beat black motorist Rodney King.

Afghanistan overthrows its communist government.

The US, Canada and Mexico sign the North American Free Trade Agreement.

Movies 'Aladdin', 'Home Alone 2: Lost in New York', 'a Few Good Men', 'Batman Returns', 'Sister Act', 'Unforgiven' and 'the Bodyguard'.

Television ‘Tequila and Bonetti’, ‘Melrose Place’, ‘Picket Fences’, ‘Hearts Are Wild’, ‘Mann and Machine’ and ‘the Tonight Show With Jay Leno’.

Music ‘Billy Ray Cyrus’s ‘Achy Breaky Heart’, Michael Bolton’s ‘When a Man Loves a Woman’, Def Leppard’s ‘Have You ever Needed Someone So Bad’ and Bonnie Raitt’s ‘I can’t Make You Love Me’.

Rather than continue this on to the year 2022, I chose to end it here for lots of reasons. Those of you who have lived the last 30 years as adults should understand why.

I sincerely hope that you enjoyed my remembrances as much as I did................

The End

About the author

At the tender age of seventeen and after years of wanting my own car that dream finally came true. Since then, I've owned by now, I'm sure well over a hundred different cars and I loved each and every one of them.

Today at 73 years of age I'm still buying, selling and trading old cars, trucks, custom accessories and used speed equipment. I attend auto swap meets and custom car shows whenever possible.

I am a man truly blessed by the Good Lord above. I am in love with life, my wife, my children, my grandchildren, my pets, my friends and family. I could live anywhere and I seen nearly all of the United States, I choose to live in Southwest Texas.

Basically I'm retired and living life to the fullest each and every day that I'm given.

www.ingramcontent.com/pod-product-compliance
Lightning Source LLC
LaVergne TN
LVHW050541160826
845677LV00011B/2125

9798815235946